jessica likes it

jessica likes it

Tiffany Quin

Ringpull

Published by Ringpull Press Ltd in 1994

Copyright © Tiffany Quin 1994

This book is copyright under the Berne convention
No reproduction without permission
All rights reserved

Ringpull Press Ltd
Queensway House
London Road South
Poynton
Greater Manchester
SK12 1NJ

ISBN 1 89805110 0
Typeset by Hewer Text Composition Services, Edinburgh
Printed in England by Clays Limited, St Ives plc

For Ed and my son, Josh.
With love and thanks.

jessica likes

sunny days

playing

shopping

christopher

boys

showing off

parties

spaghetti

dressing up

kissing

bathtime

babysitting

surprises

cuddles

teasing

winning

pass the parcel

sunny days

On a warm and sunny afternoon in early September, Jessica strolled happily along the narrow streets of London's Soho.

Jessica loved Soho; its people, its pace, its anonymity and its attitude to sex. In Soho sex was as Jessica thought it should be: honest, without pretence, a commodity to be bought and sold where the only rule is *needs must have*. She identified with that. She belonged in Soho.

Jessica adored sunny days. The streets were always busier, people happier and she was justified in wearing the Ray-Bans and skimpy clothing that made her feel sensual and exotic. So when the sun shone, Jessica tied her hair back, painted her lips red, donned her Ray-Bans and became a French film star.

Today as every day, as she walked along the busy street, she stopped at intervals to be watched. Spotting someone looking at her, especially if it was a man, she would linger, perhaps to look in a shop window or leaf through a rail of clothes, because Jessica loved to be watched. It made her feel admired. It made her feel special. Believing that people liked to watch her she gave them something to look at, something out of the ordinary, someone interesting, someone they might like to know, might even like to be.

Turning a corner she arrived at the cafe where she regularly sat. Here she would drink coffee and fantasise about the life she'd like to be living, the life she pretended to be living on bright days in Soho.

The three tables on the pavement outside the cafe were all occupied and she found herself overwhelmed with indignation, almost tearful. Didn't they understand that she'd travelled across London just to sit at one of these tables and dream away another afternoon?

She noticed the far table was occupied by a man sitting alone. Jessica cheered up a little. She wouldn't mind sharing if he was the interesting type, by which she meant the type that would be interested in her.

She hoped for the best and glided smoothly over to the table where he sat.

"Excuse me."

He lifted his eyes from his book,

"May I?"

He nodded and she smiled as he gestured towards the empty chair.

"Help yourself," he said and returned to his book.

Jessica seated herself elegantly in the chair and watched him slyly from behind her dark glasses. Even at these close quarters she had difficulty focusing on his face. She was hopelessly myopic but her vanity dictated that she remain half blind rather than wear spectacles. The Ray-Bans made it worse but it was being seen that was important to Jessica – not seeing.

He was leaning back in his seat using one hand as a visor shielding the sun from his eyes and the other to hold his book. Jessica wasn't sure she didn't catch him peep over its spine to glance at her.

She crossed her legs towards him lifting her skirt higher on her thigh.

Jessica wasn't beautiful but she did have good legs, slim and strong. He'd glanced at those too she noticed.

Jessica was having a good day.

Her favourite waiter emerged from the cafe to take her order. He was about nineteen years old, she estimated, and had that certain painful bashfulness about him that allowed Jessica to enjoy thinking he was a virgin.

"Hello," she smiled up at him expansively. He had a tendency to blush which she found both endearing and pathetic.

"Could you bring me a cappuccino, please?"

The young waiter blushed for his blush and his face turned

very red. But it wasn't until she deliberately dropped her eyes to level with his crotch that the blush reached its maximum depth of shade.

Jessica, delighting in his anguish, looked back up at his burning face. He did not meet her eyes. He had been trying not to look at her at all, not at her cleavage, or her thighs – only to catch himself gazing there over and over.

"Nothing else for now thanks." Suddenly jolting awake, he nodded in reply and fled inside.

Had Jessica not been wearing her Ray-Bans and sharing a table with a man in Soho, she might have laughed out loud but instead she maintained her expression of cool indifference.

Jessica produced a packet of cigarettes and offered one to him.

"Smoke?" she asked and tried not to look hurt when he shook his head.

He wasn't getting away with that, she thought. Jessica needed some attention.

She took one for herself and rooted, for effect, through her small, cheap, imitation Chanel shoulder bag. Then, sighing, interrupted him again.

"Excuse me, have you a light?"

He nodded and fished a lighter from his pocket. She leaned forward for him to light it for her.

While he watched the flame burn the tip she watched his face, saw his eyes glance at her breasts.

"Thank you," she said and he nodded slightly before retrieving his book and leaning back in his chair to continue reading.

Jessica was in a good mood.

There was nothing like a nice flirt mid-afternoon to make her feel good, nothing that is except a nice fuck which would definitely have been nicer but such things were rare these days. And Jessica had to take what she could.

As she drew on her cigarette she pictured him touching her, pushing his hand between her thighs under the table. She shivered and, looking over at his crotch, wondered what his cock was like.

Her thoughts were disturbed by the waiter bringing her coffee. She removed her glasses and looked straight at him again.

"Thank you."

Once again he blushed, turned and fled. This time Jessica couldn't resist smiling.

When she looked back, her temporary host was standing to leave. And after briefly smiling at her, he was gone.

Jessica rested her chin in her hands and leaned on the table to dreamily watch him walk away.

He'd liked her, she thought, shame he couldn't stay, shame she couldn't entice him into pushing his hand up her skirt beneath the table. Her cunt contracted in pleasure and she squeezed her thighs together, feeling profoundly stirred by the vision.

Jessica sighed. Being horny was a familiar sensation for her and now, as always, it was accompanied by a dull acknowledgement that it would remain unsated. For months Jessica hadn't had any sex that she'd wanted. Now she only ever came at the end of her own fingers or the tip of a vibrator.

She looked at her watch. It was nearly one o'clock.

Richard had wanted to meet her for 'lunch', to recreate those early days of passion when they had met every lunch-time to fuck and revel in the newness of one another.

It had felt exciting and romantic then but now it was as much as she could bear just to be in the same room as him, never mind have him crawl all over her.

If she took her time in winding her way home then he would have returned to work. She wanted to miss him. Of course she'd have to think of a story to explain why she hadn't been able to make it, but that wasn't a problem.

Lying had never been a problem for Jessica.

She stubbed out her cigarette, irritated now. Thoughts of Richard always brought her mood down. She hated his presence in her life and attributed every ounce of her misery to him.

He was a college lecturer and now, as she often did, she indulged in a bitter fantasy as she vaguely watched the flow of Soho passing by her table. In her fantasy she would fuck all of his students in pairs or groups of three and four until she'd been had by every one, making sure that they understood just what a little prick Richard really was. And had.

Then afterwards, and she would take particular delight in picturing this bit, they'd point at him from across the campus and elbow each other and laugh in the way that packs of young men do.

Jessica couldn't be sure whether it was the idea of humiliating Richard or the thought of having sex with groups of young men that made her vagina spasm but spasm it did.

She drained her cup of its cold coffee, left a few coins on the table and walked back down the street, feeling each stride rub her labia against the lobe of her clitoris. It was a moist manipulation; a slow-motion masturbation.

Being in Soho heightened the sensation. She walked past dark theatres advertising live-sex shows while women in minimal clothing clustered in the doorways cajoling the punters to enter.

Jessica tried to stare discreetly. How she would love to go beyond those secret doors and how she envied those who do.

It wouldn't be a bad life, she mused as she imagined herself dancing naked on a stage with hundreds of men staring up at her lecherously. Jessica had no doubts that she could do it. She'd be brilliant at it, she thought proudly. And oh yes – she saw it now in her mind's eye – she'd enjoy it.

Jessica felt in time with the street as her footsteps paced the pavement alongside the fashionable young men, filled with the energy of their media careers, or fell into time behind the clicking stilettos of the bright-haired girls and squeaking trainers of dark-eyed boys.

Jessica would have us see her as one of those bright and colourful people. She yearned to be one of them.

Now as she neared the tube station, she felt her heart sink

with disappointment as reality dismissed her fantasy of belonging and reminded her of who she was and where, and to whom, she was going.

She looked around, suddenly aware that it was plain to everyone that she didn't really belong there; that they knew she was really going home to Richard's two bedroom semi in Crouch End, their co-hab abode, their little dullnest.

Jessica quickened her step. The more distanced she felt from Soho the more desperate she became to escape it.

Her heart was racing and she felt panicky. Now she didn't want anyone to see her. She looked at her feet, walking in fear of meeting the eyes that must surely be mocking her.

Poor Cinders. Collecting her torn pride and tattered fantasy with eyes lowered and shoulders hunched she heads for home, to Richard's home.

playing

Jessica opened the gate to Richard's house with some trepidation, desperately hoping he wouldn't be in. She put her key into the door. Pushing it wide she stepped into the hallway and listened for any signs of occupation.

There were none. No music meant there was no Richard. She shut the door with a slam and called his name just to make sure. Happy and relieved at the silent response she skipped up the stairs and went directly into the bedroom.

Jessica liked her afternoons alone in Richard's house. She liked Richard's house and thought again what a shame it was that she didn't like Richard. Quickly putting the thoughts of him out of her head before they spoiled her mood she busied herself with the routine. Close the curtains, smooth the quilt, shut the door, undress, turn the light off and the lamp on. The lamp was merely decorative and gave off only a subtle red glow but she liked the way it made her skin look.

She retrieved a long thin box from her bedside drawer. It contained her Girls Best Friend vibrator. With its cold, smooth plastic surface it didn't look like a cock which was fine by Jessica. Vibrators were not cock replacements as far as she was concerned.

Jessica had a cornucopia of battery-operated dildos. Partly because she enjoyed buying them. She liked going into the shops that women rarely enter alone, and perusing the exciting contents of the wide glass-cabinets, ingenuously asking the shop assistant for help. She liked to look into their eyes as she asked what they would recommend for anal sex or if they had dual-ended dildos. Then she would handle the goods firmly, checking the weight, width and length like an expert, like a woman who knows what she wants.

The assistants rarely displayed any surprise or even interest in anything other than making a sale but Jessica knew that they were secretly impressed and that they were wishing they could be there to watch her use the tools.

She might have let them had they asked.

Jessica loved the sex she had alone. She liked the control; the power of fantasy. Alone she was safe. There was no one to please but herself. She didn't have to do anything she didn't want to. There would be no shame or disgust.

Jessica lay herself on the bed, spread her ankles to the corners and closed her eyes.

She ran her hands gently over her breasts, ribs, waist, hips, the inside of her thighs, concentrating hard on separating the sensations of touching and being touched, focusing on them individually so she could both imagine running her hands over a woman's body and having hands on her body.

She brushed lightly over her breasts and pulled at her nipples.

She loved breasts. She had slept with women just so that she could be allowed to look at and touch their breasts.

She allowed her mind free rein as it flicked from one fantasy to another. Some that had been favourites were now showing wear, others were outgrown. One or two were ever-enjoyable.

She began her fantasy by imagining thick velvet curtains being slowly drawn back to reveal a taller more beautiful version of herself in a spotlight, on a stage wearing a small black bikini.

There was a loud rumbling of throaty cheers and clapping from the men who filled the stalls below as Jessica began to dance for them. As she moved towards them the stage became a cat-walk, either side of which were lines of men looking up at her shouting for her attention. On the bed, Jessica began to slide her finger back and forth slowly over her clitoris while she kept her eyes tightly shut and her mind focused on their faces.

She switched roles for a while, from dancer to audience, so that she could watch herself as she performed her erotic ballet. Then the cat-walk faded and the stage became a towering narrow podium upon which she stood in a sea of leering jeering faces.

Jessica was a star and her fingers were moving a little faster.

The podium slowly dropped down to the audience. Now, when she knelt, they were able to reach out and touch her. Fingers from all directions pulled at the strings that held her bikini together while she writhed to the music, on her knees in the midst of them. With her arms in the air they needed no prompting to remove the flimsy articles that kept her full nudity from them.

Now she was gloriously naked and her oiled skin shimmered under the spotlight as the podium, now but two feet in diameter, began to rotate slowly.

Jessica's breath was growing heavy and her quick fingers were bringing her closer and closer to the time when she would know nothing but ecstatic pleasure for a long precious second.

The star was on all fours circling her arse in the air in time to the music with hundreds of hands sliding over her slippery body, dipping into every crack and fold. They turned her on to her back and held her legs and arms while a beautiful young man stood before her and unbuttoned his flies. He pushed his cock deep inside her and began to fuck her slowly. Then his face began to mutate into that of another, a wrinkled old man.

Jessica struggled to return to the face of the younger man but once again it changed. It was a woman, no it was Richard, the paper boy, a beard, fat, thin, black, tramp, Richard.

Jessica swore aloud. She had to concentrate. She was so close. She slid on to the floor by the bed and turning on the vibrator she jammed it between the mattress and the base. She knelt astride the jutting tool and slid her clitoris along its length and back.

It was her cock and she was fucking it with her cunt. Rocking her hips back and forth across it while holding on to the mattress for support she pretended it was Richard she was tearing into, jamming her cock up his arse over and over.

Every muscle in Jessica's body was clenched tight as she fucked across the cold plastic faster and harder until a hot fountain of warmth shot through her being as she arched her spine and received the shock of orgasm.

Deflating she slid on to the bedroom floor and lay still with her heart thumping against her chest and the last shivers of her orgasm rippling through her.

Jessica looked up at the redundant vibrator still whirring away under the mattress. She giggled at its absurdity and reached over to switch it off just in time to hear Richard's footsteps ascending the staircase.

"Shit." Jessica rolled her toys under the bed quickly and switched off the lamp. She dived beneath the quilt and feigned a deep sleep.

It wasn't from shame that she hid the evidence from Richard. She used to let him watch her do it but that was before she despised him. It was because he would want to be involved which was the last thing Jessica wanted.

"Why don't you ever want to fuck any more? Are you fucking somebody else? I love you baby. Just want to make you happy, take care of you," he would whine.

To which Jessica's response would be, "You make my skin crawl. I'm fucking the whole world. You could never make me happy. I don't need taking care of and don't bother loving me because I hate you." Except she never said it.

Instead she would tell him anything to appease him and then have to prove it to him by fucking him which only served to confound her hatred.

"Jess, are you asleep?" She heard a soft voice. Richard had entered the room.

Stupid fucking question, thought Jessica.

She could sense him bending over her, looking at her with the puppy-dog eyes that Jessica found so infuriatingly pathetic.

"I love you Jess."

I knew it. She rolled over, as if in her sleep, away from his gaze. She waited for a few seconds before opening her eyes a fraction to look at the mirrored wardrobe doors in which the whole bedroom was reflected. She was horrified to find he was naked to the waist, and in the process of removing his jeans.

Her mind began to race to find an escape route, then she felt the mattress dip under his weight as he climbed into bed beside her. Jessica froze and held her breath.

Please just go to sleep, Jessica pleaded uselessly. He was hardly there for an afternoon kip.

Jessica was angry with him for coming home unannounced and spoiling her day. What was he doing home at this time anyway? He was supposed to be at college.

Jessica resisted a shiver of revulsion as she felt a cold finger trace a line down her spine. It took all her control to stop herself from physically recoiling.

He smoothed the palm of his hand over her hip and stroked down her leg to her knee and back up along her stomach to her breast which he cupped in his small clammy hand.

Jessica lay very still, almost desperate enough to pray.

Richard moved his body in closer to hers, pressing his chest to her back. She could feel his erection rubbing against her backside.

She wanted to scream, to leap out of the bed, to tell him how he disgusted her, but confrontations with Richard were neither productive nor cathartic. They invariably resulted in a tirade of verbal abuse from Jessica and tears from Richard.

The wrath of Jessica was quite something to behold, though for the most part she managed to suppress it. Besides she hated to see Richard cry. It brought everything she loathed in him to the fore.

He was weak, pathetic and predictable.

Worse, he was just like all the rest, which according to Jessica is the worst crime a man can commit.

There were times when Jessica suspected that Richard had endeavoured to encompass into his personality everything about people, and particularly about men, that she abhorred and now this human manifestation of all despicable qualities known to

Jessica was dipping his grubby little fingers into her still moist vagina. Jessica almost groaned out loud. He was bound to take the credit for her wet pussy.

Jessica was right.

Richard was delighted.

Spurred on, he shuffled down the bed like a good lover.

As soon as his head was safely beneath the quilt Jessica opened her eyes and rolled them in exasperation. She wondered how long she could reasonably expect Richard to believe that she was still asleep.

Lying in a foetal position on her side she felt uncomfortably vulnerable to Richard's tongue but, having chosen to remain asleep, she had no option other than to allow him continued uninhibited reign over her body.

He was rimming her arse-hole when it occurred to Jessica what a shame it was she'd never mastered a control of flatulence.

She was, however, gaining some satisfaction from the fact that with his nose stuffed up her fanny, beneath fifteen togs of quilt, he must surely have been quite suffocated.

Soon, Jessica had had as much as she could take of Richard chewing and lapping at her genitals. The noise reminded her of a dog eating.

He was causing such a disturbance that Jessica felt that maintaining the farce would've aroused certain suspicion from the puppy nibbling at her labia. Taking a deep breath she turned on her back and spread her legs wide, throwing in a theatrical groan for good measure.

She could've laughed, the scene was so ridiculous, and equally she could've cried for its familiarity.

From experience she knew that the whole thing would be over a lot faster if she just faked it.

Jessica believed that men came by their ego: if you can convince them that they're an incredible fuck they cum more quickly.

Having resigned herself to letting Richard fuck her she didn't see any point in allowing his fanny-tickling exercises to continue.

She thrust her hips into the air and her cunt into his face. Reaching down she linked her fingers round the back of his neck and rammed his head between her thighs which she promptly closed around his ears and squeezed as hard as she could.

"Come on then you little bastard, work for it," she mouthed and gave angry, jerky thrusts with her pelvis that slapped him in the face.

She wanted him to drown in his own slobber.

Richard, apparently inspired by Jessica's performance, sacrificed his right to breathe and maintained his blow job with the ferocity he thought she was demanding.

Unable to bear any more she arched her back, tensed her thighs and let go an awesome cry.

This was Richard's cue to turn her over in the rough fashion that she had come to know made him feel like such a man.

Then Richard fucked her like a dog.

Which was quite appropriate because at that black moment, Jessica felt like one.

She turned her head towards the wardrobe doors and saw Richard pounding himself against her arse. He couldn't have chosen a worse time to overcome his affliction. Jessica had betted on him cumming immediately, true to form, and was devastated at this display of prowess.

"Please cum, please," she implored into the pillow as she bit it. One final thrust and he silently splashed his watery semen at her cervix.

He collapsed on top of her, crushing her to the bed beneath him, forcing the air out of her lungs before rolling over beside her. She remained limp, facing away from him, staring into the mirror at the scene within it.

"You enjoyed that didn't you baby."

Jesus Christ, now he wants praise?

"Mmmm," she replied.

"I love sex with you Jess. You're so horny. It just gets better doesn't it?" He stroked her shoulder lazily.

If you mean that my orgasms get louder and you get to push it in a few more times before you cum, then I'd say it was vastly improving.

So fucking predictable Richard.

Her eyes were blazing with the truths she would've loved to purge.

Her stomach was trembling with the effort of keeping it in.

The consequence of spilling her bile would be having to leave him, and the sad truth was that Jessica had nowhere to go and no one to go to.

It's the price Jessica's paying for the roof above her head, the price of not being alone.

It's not such a high price really, not if you're Jessica and you know you mustn't be alone.

"I love you Jess." The intonation expected a reply but she couldn't bring herself to look at him or speak to him for fear that he would read *vile* and *disgusting* in the place of the words of love for which he searched.

He pulled her shoulder, turning her over to face him, and took her chin between his thumb and forefinger. He gazed into her eyes in a way that Jessica found sickeningly sincere.

"Just want to be with you, that's all." Jessica smiled weakly at him and hoped it would suffice. He released her face, slapped her buttock and leapt out of bed with renewed energy.

"Put a nice dress on and I'll treat you to dinner."

shopping

Jessica liked the tube. What inhibited others on the tube freed
Jessica.

The searching eyes of bored travellers skipped from one face to
the next, never daring to gaze for fear of being caught, clinging on
to their anonymity as tightly as they clutched the phallic stalactites
that hung flaccidly at regular intervals from the ceiling of the
carriage.

While others averted their eyes from contact, Jessica challenged hers to be met.

For Jessica the tube held a multitude of entertainment.

Every day, somewhere between Richard's front gate and
Finsbury Park Tube Station, Jessica left herself behind. Left
behind the Jessica who let herself be pawed and gnawed at by
some creep she detested because she couldn't afford to leave
him, because she didn't have anywhere to go to or anyone to go
to; the Jessica that would rather be pawed and gnawed than leave
to go to nowhere, to meet no one; the Jessica that was scared of
the dark and being alone.

She despised this Jessica because she was weak, pathetic and
predictable, like a man. So when Jessica scurried away from the
cage that was Richard's house, she transformed into a lioness:
proud, stalking, purring, strong, sleek and magnificent.

By the time Jessica reached the corner of Richard's street, she
was ready to emerge in a blaze of self-confidence on to the high
street, a completely new woman.

A woman she liked.

On the tube she took a commanding position at one end of the
carriage, facing in. Directly in front of her was a greater spotted
teenager who Jessica instantly forgave for staring at her breasts,
after all he was only a few inches from being at eye-level with

them. He caught her watching him looking and blushed furiously. Jessica made up her mind to push them into his face at the next opportunity to see if his face could go any redder.

Next she caught a woman's eye.

She was about the same age as Jessica, maybe a little younger. She smiled in her embarrassment and looked away. Jessica was as interesting to women as she was to men. She had a quality that women admired and men feared; an overt and shameless sexuality.

Jessica had long since discovered the power of her sexuality. It was like carrying a gun. It didn't have to be fired to frighten people. It didn't have to be used in order to protect her. Its potency was rarely questioned. All she had to do was wear it, make sure it was visible then she felt safe.

You need something to make you feel safe when you trust no one.

Jessica wouldn't have been seen dead in public without her sexuality and made a point of never leaving the house without it.

Jessica's eyes returned to the same woman and caught her looking for a second time. This time she didn't smile but fixed her gaze resolutely away, giving Jessica an opportunity to look at her. She was very pretty, Jessica noted, much more so than herself which stabbed her delicate ego.

Jessica just missed being pretty, but she had learned that there was more to being desirable than being beautiful. Pretty, delicate women, however, made Jessica feel butch and unattractive. It was for that reason she held them beneath contempt, despising them for their petite feminine fragility. They enraged her those frilly, silly girls who lowered their eyes in modesty; those coy coquettes with their lacy smiles and *Ann Summers* underwear who used their big, frightened eyes to make inadequate adult boys feel like big strong men.

Jessica wanted to slap their faces.

She tried to burn her stare into the side of the woman's head, willing her to turn and look at her again so that she could glare into her big cow eyes in disgust.

But she didn't look again so when the tube pulled into the next station Jessica moved down the carriage, stopped and stood directly in front of her, a little closer than was polite. Her head held high, Jessica looked down her nose at the woman's face, just waiting for her to dare to look up and meet her eyes. When she did Jessica was waiting with a sneer.

She shook her head at her slowly with her eyes full of pity and contempt.

The young woman looked horrified to see this strange woman glaring down at her in such a way.

She couldn't have known why Jessica hated her; that Jessica felt the need to punish women like her and that it wasn't really her but what she represented.

The woman stood to leave as the train pulled into the next station.

Jessica didn't move aside for her but stretched to her full height and stood firm facing her. She grinned at the smaller woman's frightened-bunny expression and raised her hand to finger the gold chain that the woman wore around her neck. Then she dropped her hand and cupped briefly the woman's breast. Jessica laughed at her as she lurched back from Jessica's touch and fled from the carriage.

Jessica took her victim's vacated seat and chuckled to herself as she replayed her look of horror at Jessica's intrusion.

Jessica had to assert her power whenever she could.

The tube pulled in to Covent Garden Station and Jessica allowed herself to be carried towards the exit on the wave of frantic employees. Buffeted by shoulders, scratched by low-flying briefcases, whipped by open trench-coats flying in the windy tunnels, she was finally carried out on to the pavement and welcomed by crisp morning sunlight and fresh air.

As fresh as London air could be.

Jessica loved to walk around the market in the morning.

There were so many beautiful people in Covent Garden.

She glanced at her watch. She was an hour early. She would have time to walk round the stalls before meeting her friend.

She'd be on time for once, she thought. Not that it would matter if she wasn't. Chris wouldn't mind. He never minded anything Jessica did or didn't do. He made no demands on her time or affection, thought everything she did was acceptable. He was, consequently, Jessica's favourite person.

Jessica strolled around the stalls. She very rarely actually bought anything. She just liked to look and to feel a part of the beautiful crowd who appeared to just mill around all day long not doing anything in particular.

So Jessica milled too, in and around and amongst these people who fascinated her so much. The scruffy punks, the slick trendies, the dreadlocked hippies, the rich yuppies.

She wondered where they all lived; where they went to when the market closed; where they slept, ate, fucked, who they fucked and how.

Jessica was quite convinced that whatever they did it had to be better than what she did when she went home.

When she went home to feed the dog.

"Fuck," she cursed under her breath as she recalled who she was and what she did when she went home, who she fucked and how.

A fresh flush of fury knotted her stomach and the market place stopped being beautiful.

The crowd served only to taunt her about how boring and stupid she was, of how boring and stupid Richard made her feel.

He'd lied to her. He'd promised to be everything she wanted.

He was just like all the rest.

"Worse than all the rest," she said out loud to the rail of *Levis* through which she was browsing.

"I hope you're not talking about my jeans," said a voice from behind her.

The tall stall-holder was smiling down at her.

"No. Just thinking out loud," she said with a sigh.

"Penny for 'em," he asked with a look that suggested to Jessica that he wasn't at all interested in her thoughts.

"Not worth a penny," she replied.

He moved nearer until he was standing very close to her. She could smell his skin.

"Beautiful faces like yours look better with a smile." He touched her cheek with the back of his fingers.

Jessica recoiled from his intrusion. What gave this guy the right to touch her without invitation? They were all the same, she thought. All took what they wanted without asking. All thought they had a right to Jessica. She was the one in control and if she wanted him she would have him and it would have nothing to do with what he wanted.

"There's not always anything to smile about," she replied.

"A girl with a body like yours should always have something to smile about. It makes me smile," he said, looking at her breasts and smiling.

Jessica cringed.

This guy really thought he was something, she thought sneering. At the same time, though she would never have admitted it, she was flattered by his attention. Jessica was so easily flattered. It excited her. Her nipples were visibly erect.

"Cold?" he asked indicating her breasts with his eyes. Jessica found herself laughing flirtily in spite of her indignation.

"Want me to warm you up?" he offered, joking.

"What makes you think you could?"

She was challenging him.

She was the predator and he her victim. He'd picked on the wrong woman if he thought she'd be intimidated by him. She would make him put his cock where his mouth was.

"Wanna try me?" he said and it became a game of chicken to Jessica.

To back out would be to lose.

And to lose to a man was unforgivable.

"Do you come with a guarantee?" Jessica cocked her head to one side girlishly.

"We both do," he said arrogantly.

He didn't seem as intimidated by her as she'd hoped.

"I've heard that before. Empty promises in my experience," she said.

"Try me," he said smugly and leant back from her against the trestle table.

With his arms folded he looked at her, laughed and shook his head.

He thought this was all a game; that she would walk away with a giggle, she thought angrily.

He didn't know Jessica.

She reached behind him and picked up a pair of jeans from the table and held them up to his face while pressing her crotch against his knee.

"I'll try these," she said.

She saw him swallow. She sneered at him. They didn't like it when the roles were reversed.

She took his hand and led him behind the curtain of the makeshift changing room.

He followed like a lamb.

"Shut the curtain," she commanded.

He obeyed.

Jessica was feeling exhilarated.

You don't need a ring through the end of your nose when you've got a perfectly good prick for women like Jessica to pull on.

She unzipped the front of her top slowly while he stood and watched. Inviting him to do nothing but that, she slipped her top from her shoulders and let it drop to the floor.

She allowed him to look at her breasts for a moment before turning her back and sliding her leggings down to her ankles keeping her legs straight so her cunt winked at him from under her airing cheeks.

"You'll have to help me pull them over my boots," she said and signalled for him to kneel at her feet. Holding on to the rail to steady herself she waited for him to comply with her direction.

"Fuck me!" he said.

He was impressed by her body. They usually were.

He did not help her remove her leggings but swung her round to face him fiercely and kissed her hard on her mouth, pushing his whole tongue inside it, filling the entire cavity.

Jessica wanted to gag.

He was squeezing her breasts too hard and pressing her to him so tightly that she could hardly breathe.

This wasn't supposed to be happening.

It wasn't the way Jessica had planned it. He was supposed to do as she told him in exchange for what she would give him and now he was taking what he wanted without permission.

Jessica had changed her mind.

She didn't want him to paw her like this. She wanted to dress and leave.

Sadly Jessica couldn't say no. No matter how much she wanted to, she could not back out now.

What would he think of her? Just another prick tease; a weak woman without the courage of her convictions?

No, it wasn't like that, she thought as he dropped on to his knees in front her and pushed his rough chin between her thighs. She did it because she liked sex, because she was a liberated woman, because she could. She wouldn't be walked over.

He pulled her down on to the floor and pushed her on to her back. He hadn't needed to be rough. She would've done it just the same if he'd asked nicely.

He grabbed her ankles which were still bound by her leggings and held them up in the air with one hand while he bent down and lapped at Jessica from behind.

She felt ridiculous and humiliated. This was the way you held a baby when you cleaned its backside.

Jessica laughed silently at his frantic effort to bring her off.

Just for once she'd like someone to make her cum because they wanted to give her pleasure and not purely to inflate their own ego.

His mouth felt bigger than her cunt, like it had felt bigger than her face a few moments ago. She thought he might swallow her all up should he inhale sharply.

Jessica began to think of all sorts of things; of anything that would take her mind away from what was happening.

She was watching the feet pacing back and forth on the cobblestones through the inch high gap that the shoddy curtain left between it and the floor, when she was suddenly horrified by the thought of someone pulling back the curtain, revealing her in that position to all of Covent Garden.

Stirred into action, she performed her compulsory orgasm, a quieter version naturally and took the opportunity to dig her nails into his shoulders as hard as she could.

He lowered her legs and beamed at her while he wiped his shiny face with the back of his hand and spat what was presumably one of Jessica's pubic hairs into the air.

"Guaranteed!" he said triumphantly.

She tried to pull him down on top of her, partly to avoid commenting, also as a weak attempt to regain control. Somehow asking for it would mean he was respecting her wishes when he gave it to her.

And he was going to give it to her. In Jessica's experience, which was vast, men never gave anything for nothing.

He took hold of her hips in his enormous hands and clumsily turned her over on to all fours.

She should've known he was going to do that. They all did that. She submitted like a good woman, just wanting it over.

She heard the rustling of his trousers coming down and braced herself as he pushed her knees further apart.

She felt his fingers open her up to cold air then nothing. Jessica was furious. The bastard was looking at her. Why couldn't he just get on with it?

She felt his hand grip her shoulder firmly. Then he fucked her hard with his fingers, painfully twisting and turning them. Then he held them deep inside her and grabbed her whole cunt with the rest of his hand and squeezed.

"That nice?" he asked.

She wanted to grab his balls and rip them from his body in reply.

That would feel nice.

She would've prayed for it all to just be over and done with but she just wasn't the praying type so she tightened her lip and stayed silent.

He withdrew his hand and she felt the tip of his cock at her vagina.

"Go on then, you fucker," she mouthed silently and he did. He rammed himself against her cervix and Jessica lurched forward with his force. He gripped her hips again with his massive hands that almost circled her and brought her down on him, over and over.

Jessica gasped as he slapped her buttocks against his stomach, sliding her up and down his cock.

He was making her fuck it. Jessica almost let a tear escape as he got faster and more frenzied, plunging and pounding her body.

She bit down on her lip to stop the angry tear from falling.

Then he pulled out of her and she felt warm drops on her buttocks and back.

He dropped her hips and let her sink into a ball on the square of carpet beneath them. She was exhausted.

The bastard came on my back. She was fuming, suspecting it was less to do with respect for her safety than a canine marking of territory, like pissing on a lamppost.

Jessica felt marked and pissed on.

"Have you got something to wipe that off with?" she asked him.

"Yeah, sure, sorry," he said, breathlessly and she felt him mop her up with a corner of the curtain, which she thought a charming touch.

"Thanks," she said dubiously.

Reaching for her clothes she began to dress quickly as his sweat on her skin began to freeze.

He took the cue and pulled up his tracksuit bottoms.

Jessica didn't meet his eyes once.

"Feel better now?"

"Oh please," she whispered and glanced briefly at his face which she wanted to claw from his head.

"Yes thank you," she said politely.

Silent dressing.

"So when are you coming to see me again?" he asked confidently. Jessica felt dumbstruck that he should dare ask her that after all she'd just been through.

"I'll drop by next Wednesday," she said.

"Give me your phone number?" he demanded.

Who did he think he was, Jessica wondered as she lied?

"I don't have one. Give me yours. I'll ring you."

He nodded his head and bent down to kiss her.

If he could have sensed a fraction of the loathing that Jessica felt for him at that moment, he wouldn't have been so cocky, for Jessica was realising she possessed a potential to kill.

The effort of remaining composed while he filled her mouth with his tongue again took all the discipline she could muster. It was all she could do not to spit out the saliva he left behind there into his face when he pulled away.

She swallowed it and turned her back to hide the retch as she felt it slip down her throat.

He peeked out from behind the curtain and stepped out.

Jessica wiped her mouth, tidied her hair and straightened her clothes before stepping out after him.

There was a small cluster of potential customers gathered around the trestle table fingering the jeans. They looked up at Jessica as she handed back the *Levis* she hadn't tried on. She tried not to care what was on their minds or wonder whether they'd heard anything or not.

She watched him write something on a receipt and place it into a plastic carrier bag together with the jeans she'd handed him.

"Nice fit," he said and not in the least bit discreetly.

"Yes, thanks," she said dryly, "See you Wednesday."

"I'm looking forward to it already," he leered after her as she turned out of his stall.

At a hurried but steady pace she made her way towards the outskirts of the market, feeling oppressed by the crowds of people that pushed and jostled against her; that held her up; that kept her restrained against her will.

She could feel his sperm on her back, staining her skin. She was paranoid that with people so close they might smell him on her. She felt so very dirty.

She gave one final push and the crowd expelled her from its heaving nucleus allowing her air and relief.

She headed straight towards a bin with the intention of discarding the carrier bag she still clutched but as she lifted it to drop it in, she reconsidered.

They were good jeans. Why shouldn't she have got something out of it? She rummaged round inside it until she found the receipt which she promptly tore up into a hundred tiny pieces that she sprinkled into the wind ceremoniously.

The next most urgent task was to get to a bathroom. She dipped into the first cafe she came to.

As she wiped her back, her arse and all around her vagina with wads of damp toilet roll, Jessica didn't ask herself if it had been worth it to prove her point. She thought about how she would never be able to go back to the market again. How she had forgone one of her most favourite pastimes and for what?

She wetted the fifth wad of tissue paper and resumed the rubbing of her red raw flesh.

Finally satisfied that she was as clean as she was going to get without taking a bath, she dressed herself, left the privacy of the cubicle and tidied up her face in the mirror.

She smiled at her reflection and shrugged her shoulders.

"Pretty is as pretty does."

christopher

Jessica had taken the long route, around the back of the market, to the cafe where Chris would have been waiting for over forty minutes.

Chris was Jessica's best friend.

Best and only.

Jessica liked to appear to have friends, hating to seem friendless, but believed the level of commitment required to maintain sexless relationships was totally unrealistic. They simply asked too much. How could Jessica be expected to be honest, reliable, dependable and trustworthy in a world where everyone lies and you can't trust or depend upon anybody?

Jessica found it simpler to be reliably dishonest, honestly untrustworthy and to fuck all and sundry in order to side step the confusing platonic issue.

The philosophy was basic; you meet, get on, lie about who you are and when you eventually disappoint them, you flatter and fuck them in the hope they'll forget what a phoney they discovered you to be. Then they'll either fall in love with you and become your slave until you get bored with them or they'll walk out of your life.

To Jessica, friendships were useful assets only until they became responsibilities at which point they became disposable. Her family, for the same reason, had been disposed of several years before. The only hiccup in the system was that Jessica quite often found herself friendless and alone but she appeased herself with the fact that unlike most she was answerable to no one.

Jessica liked to travel light.

Chris made no demands on her time or energy and never criticised anything she did, even when what she did hurt him which it often did.

Jessica also liked the idea of him. He wanted to work in film. She romanticised him as a struggling artist and fantasised that one day he would be famous and so would she, if only by proxy.

Having put all thoughts of her rendezvous at the stall to the back of her mind she entered the cafe and scanned the tables for Chris's skinny frame.

He was sitting at a corner table at the far end of the room reading a book with his back to her.

She crept up behind him, slipped her arms around his neck and kissed his cheek.

"Sorry I'm late Chris."

"I never expected anything else," he said grinning.

And he hadn't.

He stood and hugged her to his chest warmly.

It's nice to be held by someone who genuinely likes you and who asks nothing from you.

She hugged him back tightly and for a fraction longer than necessary which he noticed.

"Are you okay?" he asked her tenderly.

Chris really cared. He cared much more than Jessica wanted to know.

"Nothing a dead boyfriend wouldn't fix," she said wearily.

They sat down opposite one another.

"So how is our Dick?" Chris smirked.

"He needs a good fisting," she said in reply and gestured violently with her clenched fist, which made him laugh.

"I could talk to someone for you," he joked.

Jessica smiled at her friend sweetly and fluttered her eyelashes comically.

He would have done anything for one of her smiles, her affectionate little touches, a kind word or a gentle look and Jessica knew it.

Of course she knew he was in love with her but that was okay. Jessica didn't mind.

Chris could see that Jessica was upset about something but

he wasn't going to push her into telling him. He knew from experience that Jessica didn't like to be pushed.

"If it gets too much you could always come and stay with me for a while you know," he said hopefully.

Nothing would have made him happier.

"Just to get some space," he added, to ensure that she didn't read anything into his offer that might make her feel imposed upon.

"Space? Chris darling, you live in a six by ten bedsit." Jessica laughed at the wounded expression he mimicked to mask his disappointment and embarrassment.

"Thanks anyway," she said.

It had been all right for her when she'd first moved to London and needed somewhere to stay, he thought sulkily.

That was two years before, which made Chris a record for Jessica. The longest period of time she'd ever known anyone. This was down to Chris, not Jessica. He knew his place and had not once stepped out of it.

"Well, maybe if it gets really bad." Jessica twinkled her eyes at him playfully. He cheered up instantly and signalled over to the waitress for two coffees.

"What have you been buying?" Chris asked spotting her bag.

Jessica's face fell into a frown and she reached round to the small of her back to scratch the infected spot.

"Oh just some jeans. The creep who sold them to me was all over me so I put my hand on his bollocks and said we could use his changing room if he wanted. You should've seen his face. He was terrified. He couldn't get me out of there quick enough."

They both laughed at the scene Jessica described and for Jessica that was exactly as she would remember it from then on.

Chris was always impressed by Jessica's antics. She seemed so strong and confident, so sure of herself, so unlike him.

The waitress brought their coffees to the table.

Jessica saw Chris look down her blouse as she lifted the cups and saucers from the tray. The pretty young waitress smiled at him and he back at her before she left them alone again.

Jessica felt a stab of jealousy.

Any woman in Chris's life was a threat to her. As long as he wanted her more than anyone else she could keep him where she wanted him, waiting for her. All she had to do was to give him little tasters every now and then to keep his mouth watering.

Jessica needed to have something to fall back on in case all else should fail and that something was Chris.

He was an investment, a safety net that needed regular maintenance.

But there was more to it than that.

Chris was the only person that Jessica suspected had ever truly cared for her and although she didn't know how to respond to anything as pure as love, she couldn't bring herself to let it go. So Chris remained in the wings like an understudy waiting for a chance to prove himself.

Chris had noticed that Jessica's face had fallen and knew why. He regretted his minute flirtation. He knew how possessive she was.

So scathing had she been of his girlfriends in the past, so demanding did she become of his time when he had one, so overtly sexual was she with him whenever they were around and so ferocious the ritual battling she provoked until he gave up and got rid of them or they left him unable to cope with her bitchiness, that Chris no longer bothered with other women.

It just wasn't worth upsetting her.

He didn't mind. If Jessica could become jealous of other women in his life, didn't that mean that she must really care for him? It was the only clue she gave him and so he held on to it tightly.

"What an odd looking girl," Chris said, pulling a face in an attempt to smooth things over.

"Really, I thought she was just your type," she said.

"Nah, too tall and skinny for me. I hate gawky looking women."

"Liar, if you'd leaned any closer to her tits you'd have fallen down her blouse." Jessica was laughing but Chris could hear the spite.

"What tits?" he laughed, ignoring her undertone.

They both sipped their coffee.

"How's the writing going?" Chris asked mainly to ease the atmosphere.

"Okay," she replied non-commitally.

Jessica hadn't written anything in five years and only then a ten minute play for an A-level project at college and a handful of angst poetry but it had been enough for Jessica to identify herself as a writer.

It served her ego well and gave her something to bullshit about at parties.

She was still avoiding a circle of people to whom she'd once bragged of a five novel contract that she'd signed with a large publishing company.

It had made her feel good at the time but they had insisted on hounding her about the publication date of her debut novel. The crunch came when one of them mentioned they had a friend who used to work at the same company and that she should meet her.

Jessica had agreed, foolishly she thought in retrospect. It had taken the publisher friend less than ten minutes to suss her out as a fraud.

She moved south of the river shortly after.

"You're miles away today," Chris said softly as Jessica played with the froth of her cappuccino.

She jumped awake.

"I'm sorry Chris, I am. It's just this Richard thing," she offered in excuse of her silence.

"Wanna talk?" Chris hoped he sounded casual and tried not to look disappointed when she shook her head.

"I'd rather go for a stroll?" she suggested chirpily.

"I can't. I'm working at the restaurant this afternoon. I've got to go soon. Sorry Jess."

And he really was.

She would've linked his arm as they strolled and laughed and chatted. He could've pretended gloriously that they were lovers.

If only for a short time.

He saw Jessica's disappointment and it devastated him so much that he considered throwing in his job just to be able to do what she wanted; to make her smile.

But he had rent to pay.

Fifteen minutes later, he stood reluctantly and pulled his jacket on.

Jessica stayed seated. She was sulking. She would have been happy for Chris to throw in his job to keep her happy. Moreover, she expected it.

"Shall I phone you at the weekend? I'm not working then and we could go out for the day, into the country or something."

"If you want." Jessica was angry at him for abandoning her at a time when she needed him.

"Don't give me a hard time Jessica," he said in a tiresome voice.

"I'm not," Jessica defended.

"Well cheer up then," he said and kissed her cheek.

"Yeah, okay. Bye."

The pain of seeing her angry with him made tears well in the corners of his eyes. He knew that the next time they met she wouldn't even remember this and yet it hurt him terribly.

Jessica sat for a little while, feeling sorry for herself, feeling lonely and just the tiniest bit guilty.

She left the cafe soon after Chris but not before crumbling the young waitress with a bitter glance.

Careful to give the market a wide birth she wandered out on to the street.

Jessica didn't know where she was going, not now, not ever.

Once again she found herself wandering without purpose or direction.

In rare and brief moments of illumination, Jessica knew that this aimlessness summed up her life completely and it utterly depressed her.

For the majority of the time she had herself convinced that she was free; unencumbered by the restrictive conventions of society; experiencing life, exploring places that most people were scared to go.

She was satisfied with this perception of herself.

It made her behaviour seem reasonable.

She existed within the conscious realms of her own subjective reality. A kingdom of reality of which Jessica was Queen, Dictator and God.

The problem is that a dictator needs people to dictate to, a queen needs subjects to rule over, and a god needs deluded and desperate souls to watch over and offer promises that can't be met. And Jessica lives alone in her reality.

Without mirrors there are no reflections and without reflections there is only Jessica.

Jessica and the truth.

She sat on a bench on a grass verge by the side of a busy road.

She watched the scene that was being played out in front of her, superfluous to it, not existing as a part of it only as an onlooker.

In front of her was a young mother with her daughter. They held hands and laughed as the girl skipped happily along with her long fair hair bouncing and curling. They crossed the road heading straight towards Jessica's bench.

The little girl looked at her and smiled sweetly.

Jessica swallowed an ocean and smiled back briefly.

Following them with her eyes as they shrank into the horizon, she thought jealously of how pretty the child had been; how young and innocent and happy she had looked.

She swallowed another ocean.

Lighting a cigarette and inhaling deeply she filled her lungs with the noxious fumes she despised.

Jessica was sinking: there on the bench breathing the carcinogens from the cars and her cigarette, alone, unreflected and filled with self-pity and despising herself for it.

A car drew up at the traffic lights. There was loud music filtering through the open window on the passenger side. Jessica saw a beautiful thirty-ish woman throw back her head in laughter and wrap her arms around the thirty-ish man in the driving seat. She was kissing him and he was laughing, wrestling her out of the way as the lights changed to green and they roared off into their lives together.

A second choking twist.

Jessica closed her eyes to blot out the radiant faces of couples in love or dancing children safe in the warm security of their parents' love.

To Jessica they all belonged to the same world, some other world to which she was not privy.

They all belonged somewhere and to someone.

Jessica was consumed with a bitter ache of an ancient grief. She had allowed herself to be alone and now she was paying the price. Even Richard's company was better than her own, she thought. Or was it? She wasn't sure.

"Fuck it" she groaned.

Then there was that childish feeling of being watched from above. She raised her eyes to the heavens and said, "Fuck you too."

She flicked the butt of her cigarette into the road and watched it for a while as it pinwheeled under the passing vehicles, spraying embers across the tarmac.

"Let's get pissed." she said finally and resolutely.

She smiled as she heard her own voice.

"You're losing it," she sang.

Marching purposefully down the street Jessica thought again

that she might be insane though she suspected talking to herself was the least significant symptom.

"First bar I come to." She lifted her chin defiantly against the world and squared her shoulders like a proud matador entering the bullring.

God help the bull.

boys

Jessica hadn't felt like a brave matador when she'd first entered the pub. It had been filled with early drinkers wearing fashionable clothes and talking in loud voices about things that Jessica didn't know about.

She felt insignificant and stupid as she sat all alone with her vile, throat-scorching drink which made her shiver in revulsion and screw up her face against every sip.

She was doing her best to look as if she were waiting for somebody, someone wonderful or important who was late. She sipped her scotch and peered out of the window with a frown and a sigh that asked impatiently, *Where is he?*

She looked at her watch again, lit another cigarette and asked herself why she didn't have anyone to meet.

The door opened and Jessica looked up expectantly as she had each time someone had opened the door. It wasn't her late lover, her expression said to anyone who might see.

She'd hate anyone to think that she was there alone because she had no one to be there with.

Jessica returned to the bar a third time and ordered another drink.

"Large scotch please," she spoke confidently and glanced at the door again.

The same barman had served her on each of her visits to the bar and Jessica felt the need to excuse her solo drinking. She didn't want him thinking she was a lonely sad alcoholic.

"You haven't seen a tall guy with short dark hair in a dark green suit come in have you?" she enquired of the barman.

"Sorry love," he said without looking at her.

"He's always bloody late," she said affecting an exasperated tone, paid for her drink and returned to her table contented that she'd excused herself for at least another half an hour.

Jessica, not being a regular drinker, had begun to feel the alcohol in her brain half way through her second drink and now half way down her third she was feeling warm and slightly numb.

And numb was pleasant.

Tapping her foot to the music she watched as three girls got up to dance on the small floor set aside for the purpose.

Jessica would've liked to have danced too but not alone. Maybe when the dance floor was full then no one would notice that she was alone.

She drained her glass.

Maybe if she was drunk enough she wouldn't care whether they noticed or not.

The door was opened again and Jessica, more for curiosity this time, glanced up to see it close behind two men. Boys really, Jessica thought as she watched them push their way through the crowd to the bar.

One of them in particular Jessica found very attractive. Whether it was the alcohol or the fact that the bar was by now very busy wasn't clear but Jessica began to feel less conspicuous, more confident and a little playful.

She edged through to where they stood at the bar waiting with many others to be served, inching along until she was standing directly behind the one she found attractive. She had an over-whelming urge to feel him up.

She wanted to dance, have a good time, get utterly drunk and have a new boyfriend for the night to help her forget the older one she already had.

Someone pushed past Jessica and, taking advantage of the opportunity, she pressed her body right up against the boy at the bar.

He turned with a scowl that disappeared when he saw the offender was Jessica in a tight zip-down top.

"Sorry," she mouthed and smiled sweetly.

"Busy isn't it?" he shouted over the music.

"Yes," Jessica shouted back.

Close-up the boy wasn't as good looking as Jessica had first thought but he was smiling at her and nudging his mate and Jessica wasn't feeling picky.

He moved up to create a space for her at the bar. She nodded in thanks.

The mate was served first and after ordering their drinks he waved over to Jessica.

"What are you drinking?"

"Whisky and coke," she yelled back thinking that she better make the next one a long one as she began to feel a bit light and hot.

"Cheers," she said as he handed her the glass and smiling coyly but suggestively she pulled away from the bar.

If they were interested then they would follow her. If not, she'd try someone more willing.

She positioned herself carefully so that she could both watch the action on the dance floor and keep an eye on her two boys who seemed to be taking their time coming.

They probably needed a little more enticement she decided and began to stare at them, willing them to turn.

The sharp edges of her thinking gone, she considered that she might have the power to think them into doing whatever she wanted them to.

She concentrated hard.

It was working she was sure it was.

Any minute now.

After a few seconds of failure, Jessica gave up and went to the ladies.

The fluorescent tube of the toilet was not the most flattering of lighting. Jessica was horrified by what she saw in the mirror; pale and blemished skin, mascara blacked lines beneath her eyes and limp tangled hair.

How had she got into a state like this?

She spoke to a young girl who was brushing her hair beside her. "Can I borrow that after you?"

"Sure," the girl said and handed the brush over before returning to her preening in the mirror, which didn't seem to make her look bad.

Her flawless skin and teenage breasts burned Jessica painfully in the gut as she looked at her own haggard reflection.

"You haven't got any lipstick have you?" Jessica asked.

"No, sorry."

"No I don't suppose you need it," Jessica said sardonically and, still with her glass, shut herself into a cubicle.

Sitting on the closed lid with her feet up against the door she decided she was too drunk and remembered why she didn't drink. It was because she always drank too much. Other people knew when to stop, why couldn't she?

Her head span and her stomach threatened an uprising.

Lifting the toilet seat Jessica bent her head over the bowl. Careful to hold her hair out of the way with one hand she pushed the fingers of the other into her mouth and pressed on the back of her tongue expertly.

Her stomach emptied with the minimum of fuss and splashed around the porcelain bowl. She flushed the chain, blew her nose and felt much better.

Jessica had been self-inducing vomiting for as long as she could remember. She was very skilled. Sometimes she only had to look at a toilet bowl and think "vomit" to rid herself of whatever it was she wanted ridding from her stomach.

She finger-cleaned her teeth, gargled a few times with the last mouthful of her drink and feeling like a new woman headed straight for the dance floor.

Jessica had no inhibitions now as she bounced and sweated amidst lots of bouncing and sweating people.

She closed her eyes feeling at one with them and the music and the universe. Then opened them again quickly to stop the whirling pits that removed the floor from beneath her feet.

As she looked up she noticed the not-as-handsome-as-she'd-first-thought boy dancing in front of her and smiling broadly, with the one who'd brought her a drink dancing just behind him.

She knew they'd come eventually.

"What's your name?" He shouted into her ear.

"Jessica."

"Jessica?"

"Yeah"

He told her their names but Jessica wasn't interested so when she didn't hear the first time she just smiled, nodded and carried on dancing to the music which grew louder and more raucous.

It wasn't long before Jessica crossed the sexual barrier and ended up snogging with them both, passing from one to the other and laughing wildly while they groped her breasts and felt up her cunt.

They were laughing too.

There were more drinks, more vomiting, more dancing and more laughing.

Jessica was having wonderful time.

She was young again, and single. She was beautiful and sexy with two attentive boys at her side and, apart from the odd billow of nausea, what more could she ask for?

Of course it would be useful if she could regain control over her balance, she thought as she was yanked up by her new friends from the floor where she'd fallen for the second time. But she didn't care.

And that was what was so great about being drunk. For once in her life, she absolutely didn't care what anybody thought of her.

Jessica threw her arms in the air in celebration of her mood and lurched forward to embrace her friends, but misjudging their distance completely, fell face down at their feet.

Lying on the hard wet wooden floor didn't feel so bad, she thought and let her eyes close. She'd get up in a minute.

Jessica, unaware of anything but her own stupor hadn't realised that she was being observed.

Finally it seemed that the management had decided that Jessica had enjoyed herself enough.

"Come on love, up you get."

"What are you doing?" Jessica mumbled as she felt herself being hoisted to a standing position.

She squinted through bloodshot eyes to find herself in the arms of a man wearing a black suit and bow tie.

Jessica was very confused. Had she done something wrong?

She shrugged the bouncer off her angrily but he followed and taking her arm tried to lead her from the dance floor.

"Fuck off," she shouted.

It was all she could manage.

The next thing she knew she was being escorted, supported on either side by her two young friends, out of the pub.

The fresh night air was delicious on her clammy skin but breathing it in deeply had a strange affect on her and she found herself vomiting involuntarily on to the pavement.

"Sorry," she said to the boys as she wiped her mouth with the back of her hand. "I think I need to go home."

"You'll be all right," said one of them.

It was the first time she'd heard either of their voices and was surprised how high it was pitched. *Surely they weren't that young?*

Jessica sat down on the pavement and leaned against the cold wall. She definitely needed to be in bed.

"I've got to go home," she groaned.

"Do you need a lift?" one of them said.

"Are you old enough to drive?" she asked with her eyes closed. It was only when her eyes were open that she felt dizzy.

"Come on then."

They helped her to her feet and began walking her to the car which was parked in an alley about two hundred yards from the pub.

They leaned her against their Datsun Cherry while they went for a piss against the wall.

Jessica could hear them talking but it was too much effort to

41

concentrate on what they were saying. All she had to do was keep her eyes closed and she'd be okay.

"There you go girl," one of them said and held open the back door for her.

She felt herself being gently cajoled into the back seat of the car. She was relieved to be sitting down and out of the freezing breeze. Someone climbed in the back with her and began kissing her dry mouth roughly. Jessica flapped her hand around his face as though waving off an irritating gnat.

"Look, I just want to go home," she whined.

"We'll take you in a bit," the voice replied and resumed sucking at her face.

Then she felt him tugging at her leggings. Jessica groaned and rolled her eyes as she realised through her fog what was happening.

"I'm not in the mood, just want to sleep," she said but he was quite insistent and Jessica was too weak to fight. She felt a draught across her thighs as he peeled her leggings from them. Then an arm in the crook of her knee lifted her leg into the air.

Jessica knew what was coming next and she didn't really care as long as they took her home soon.

He fiddled with his cock near her cunt trying to find the right hole for it. Then discovering her vagina tight and dry he spat onto his fingers to wet her before plunging in.

Over and over he rocked against her, crushing her head into the door painfully.

Then he was done and off her and it was over.

Now she could go home.

She attempted to sit up and someone helped her, helped turn her over on to her stomach. She felt her hips being heaved upwards, hands spreading her buttocks, a finger up her arse, maybe two.

"No," Jessica said as firmly as she could which wasn't very.

"Why not?" came back a whisper.

"Just don't, okay." Her voice sounded weak. It was all she could do to speak.

She felt the tip of a penis against her arse-hole and tried not to tense. She knew it would hurt more that way.

"What the fuck are you doing in there man, I'm freezing my balls off out here. Hurry up," said a voice from outside the car.

"Fuck off will you, you've had yours," said the voice from behind her. "Have you ever had it up your arse before?"

Jessica would, had she not been so drunk, have told him that she'd had more little pricks up her arse than he had years to his life.

Without waiting for a reply he spat on his hand and wiped it down the crack of her arse.

For some reason *that* wounded Jessica more than when he rammed himself against her so hard that she lunged forward and hit her head on the car door.

Jessica gasped in pain as she felt him tearing her apart.

"You're hurting me," she pleaded. She wasn't fighting, the least he could do was be gentle.

"Shut the fuck up slag," he panted and gave her a sharp deep jab with his prick that made her gasp in pain again.

"Bastard," she whispered through her teeth furiously.

It seemed such a long time before he eventually came and Jessica's anus burned.

Feeling comparatively sober she tried to kneel up slowly, but before she'd completed the task she found herself being dragged by her waist from the car and dropped on to the gritted tarmac of the road.

The stones stung her knees and elbow as she landed heavily and awkwardly.

Then all at once the sound of car doors slamming, engine roaring and tyres screeching burst into the night. Then she was alone, in silence, on her knees and naked from the waist down.

She squinted around in the dark for any sign of her leggings.

There was none.

"Bastards." She let out a sob.

Jessica was crying.

But men did not make Jessica cry. She made *them* weep.

It was written.

Jessica wrote it.

She clenched her fists and punched the gravel, pounding it over and over, shivering with cold and rage.

"You stupid, stupid bitch. You got pissed and you let them. You let them, again." The words escaped her throat in deep and strangled growls. This was the voice of Jessica's rage, stirring like molten lava deep within her. Glowing rivers of pain forgotten until sparked by fresh assault. An ancient rage that dwelled in dark, secret caverns.

It scorched her; scarred and choked her with unreasoned fury at herself.

It wasn't that she didn't blame the men, more that she had come to expect nothing more from them.

She'd been having sex that she didn't want for as long as she could remember. She had come to accept it as normal.

Any man can stick it in Jessica. There's only one rule: that he knows he's having sex with Jessica only because Jessica's chosen to let him. That Jessica is in control.

Now she had broken her own rule. She had lost control and become vulnerable and was furious with herself for giving them the power. She knew what men did with power.

Jessica was never going to get drunk ever again.

Totally absorbed in her own self-loathing she didn't notice the car that had turned into the alley, not until her senses were bombarded with bright lights, burning rubber and exhaust fumes. Jessica suddenly knew it was going to hit her and she froze, unable to do anything but wait for the moment of impact, but it swerved away from her at the last moment, sending a spray of tiny stones and dust into her eyes.

"Fucking slag," came a shout from the car.

It was them.

She ducked reflexively as she saw something flying towards her head from the car, before they screamed off into the night for a second time.

Jessica was still trembling with shock a minute later, when she heard male voices in the distance getting louder.

Panicking should they see her half naked, she ran towards a parked car and crouched behind it waiting for them to come and hopefully go.

Her heart banged against her chest as the loud drunken-sounding voices laughed and joked and swore at each other just a few metres from where she hid. She pressed herself tight into the car body.

She felt so small hiding there, small, frightened, stupid and ashamed.

They were almost upon her.

It was at that point Jessica realised the car behind which she was hiding must be theirs. She didn't recall seeing any other vehicles in the alley.

She shivered as she imagined them seeing her like that and made a dash for the industrial skip that stood at the bottom of the alley. There were no street lights and they were further away than Jessica had guessed so she made her escape unnoticed.

Jessica watched them pile into the car and all but cried in relief at what she saw lying on the road in the beam of their headlights. It was her leggings that they had thrown at her.

She almost felt grateful to the boys and, as soon as the car had gone and she was sure that no one else was coming, she made a dart for them, running back behind the bin to pull them over her freezing legs to protect her modesty and hide her shame.

The shame of having let them beat her.

Jessica wiped the tears and mascara from her face and with them the painful truth of the reality that was too much to bear. Combing her knotted hair through with her fingers and drawing a deep breath, she stepped on to the street.

For Jessica there was only one thing worse than letting a

man get the better of her and that was people knowing that they had.

Jessica thought that if people knew, they would blame her, say she had it coming, deserved all she got. Or worse, she might be pitied.

She despised them. What did they know? she would ask angrily. What did anyone know?

Jessica understood that no one had a right to pain unless they had been through what she had. If anyone wanted to know about pain, they ought to ask her. She wanted to slap the miserable for being weak and jealously slash those that were happy for being able to be.

As her aberration shifted from herself to the rest of the world where she thought it belonged, where it was safe, she began to feel a little better.

It's hard being the only sane person in the world.

Jessica hailed a cab to take her home, back to Richard.

"Off to your boyfriends?" the driver shouted to her over his shoulder.

Jessica winced against the pain in her arse as she sat ignoring him, pretending to be asleep.

She had a lot to think about before she got home, like concocting a credible story to explain the condition of her clothes and breath to Richard. And so in closing her eyes she hoped to dissuade the driver from making any further intrusion into her concentration.

She became aware of a stinging sensation emitting from her hand and, lifting it to her face for inspection, she saw it was grazed and bleeding from where she'd punched the gravel.

"Shit. This is going to have to be a good one," she whispered, frowning, and began running through some possibilities.

She considered mugging but Richard would want to involve the police. He was such an upright citizen.

She decided on being hit by a car, someone giving her a stiff brandy for medicinal purposes and being taken to casualty for a check-up. The hospital had discharged her saying that she'd just suffered a bit of shock and that she was fine.

Satisfied and quite pleased with her re-creation of the evening, she sank into the leather seat of the hackney cab and let the growl of the diesel engine comfort her.

The taxi pulled up outside the house.

"You're home love," the driver's voice woke her.

Her head was aching and she longed to be in bed with soft quilt surrounding her and sleeping a deep dreamless sleep.

The car door slammed behind her.

Walking round to his open window she pulled a ten pound note from her pocket and handed it to the driver.

"Been a long night has it love?."

Fucking moron, she thought, disregarding him completely.

He handed over her change and she scowled at him in disgust of his entire race.

She spun round haughtily and went into the house.

"Richard," she called in an affected, vulnerable voice.

There was no answer but the soft, regular thudding of a bass rhythm floated down the stairs from the bedroom informing her of his whereabouts.

She walked through the dark living room and into the kitchen.

Opening the fridge she took a carton of fresh orange juice and emptied it thirstily. The alcohol had dehydrated her.

Making her way up the stairs she rehearsed her elaborate script and adopting an appropriate expression of woe she made her entrance.

"Jess, where have you been?" Richard leapt up from the bed.

The fact that he looked so worried irritated her. Did he think she was a child who couldn't look after herself?

She stood in the doorway, covered her face with her hands, and let out a sob.

Richard responded predictably, rushing to comfort her.

"Jesus you look terrible. What's wrong? What's happened?" Jessica's tears began to freely flow and they weren't all crocodile.

His arms and his sincere concern had tapped her genuine sadness and need for comfort and reassurance.

"Oh Richard." She collapsed into his arms and he carried her over to the bed where they sat, he rocking her slightly against his chest while she described in full detail her traumatic accident.

He hummed sympathetically in the right places and displayed the correct degree of shock, fear and worry. In short, he swallowed it, as she had known he would.

Whilst despising him for his gullibility she reluctantly relished being held and rocked so tenderly.

She nuzzled her face against his gentle kisses, closed her eyes and curled up tighter into his chest, wishing that she might become small enough to feel safe and protected there.

Then it occurred to her. He was trying to take advantage of her vulnerability. He thought she was weak. Her tears were making him feel like a man. It was turning him on. He just wanted to fuck her.

Like they all did.

She whipped herself around to face him and kissed him hard on his mouth, passionate, with loathing.

Yes she'd fuck him. That's what he wanted. What else was she good for?

She pulled her clothes from her body and sat astride him. Reaching for his erection roughly, she plunged herself down on him hard. The squeal that he mistook for passion was Jessica's agony as she speared her battered insides with his prick. Then again and again as she lifted and plunged on to him.

She looked down at his contorted face as he came and hated him. She wanted to spit at him, slap that stupid expression from his face, cut it off with a knife.

She lifted herself slowly from his shrivelling penis, biting down to resist crying out in pain.

She considered sitting on his face and making him swallow the mixed cum of the two other men that had emptied themselves into her body that day but she was sore.

She fell on to the bed beside him.

Richard said nothing, just lay there panting.

Jessica couldn't bear the thought of him talking to her so she said "Goodnight," and turned on her side with her back to him. She cringed as he spooned his body around hers tightly.

"Love you," he whispered.

"I know," she replied and switched out the light.

showing off

Jessica's loathing of Richard grew into monstrous proportions over the next few weeks.

Everything about him set her teeth on edge. The noisy way he ate, his snoring, the way he said her name, the music he listened to, his clothes, his thoughts, his job, his face.

Richard could barely open his mouth in Jessica's presence without eliciting a violent response from her.

Jessica was like a loose electric cable sparking on a wet floor.

And Richard was very unhappy. For which Jessica hated him more.

"Why are you so bloody miserable all the time?" she would ask him.

"Why do you get at me all the time?" he would ask in reply.

"Because you're so bloody miserable all the time," she would finish. Then he would sulk and she would fume the evening away in front of the television until bedtime when they would crawl into their designated quarter of the bed leaving the space in the middle wide enough for the ghost of the couple who used to lie there.

If Richard snored then Jessica would punch him hard to wake him and lie awake long after he had returned to sleep to think about how much she hated him and how she was going to leave him and have her freedom back.

She dreamed about being a single girl, doing whatever she wanted. She could see it all so clearly, the way it would be. She would sleep with whomsoever she wanted and flirt with the whole world if she so desired without having to later console a wounded boyfriend. She would flit from one lover to the next as she wanted. They would all fall in love with her and try to possess her but she would just laugh and flit off to the next fancy.

But Jessica had never been a single girl. She left her mother's home straight into the arms of her first adult boyfriend at fifteen and her many relationships since then had each merged into the next. But she had never acknowledged a pattern and blanked out the truth: Jessica was afraid to be without a lover.

And that was why she remained. Because there was no one better for her to go to.

Thinking about some of these things, Jessica lay in bed waiting for Richard to leave for work so she could get up.

When the front door slammed behind him, she wondered what she had to get up for. Even the party they were going to that night loomed darkly over her, because he was going to be there too.

Richard had obtained the exclusive invitation from a friend of his who had been unable to go. She remembered how excited she had been when she'd learned that there would be celebrities there. Then Richard had started talking about autograph hunting and taking his camera.

He was going to humiliate her.

She lit a cigarette – more because Richard hated her smoking in the bedroom than because she wanted one – and imagined herself at the party, mingling with lots of famous people, and Richard with his camera. She dropped ash on his pillow and then crushed the lit end into it where his face would've been, burning a hole into the linen.

Swinging her legs on to the floor she trudged into the bathroom wearing the baggy T-shirt that she'd taken to sleeping in. Then had a long shower and a wank to kill time.

As she sat at the kitchen table eating toast and staring out of the window at the drizzle, she mused at how she'd stayed with Richard so long. This was the second October she'd spent in his house, and definitely the last, she resolved.

The phone rang. She picked up the receiver.

"Hello?"

"Hi Jess, it's me." It was Richard.

"Hi," she said without emotion.

"We need to talk." Jessica lost her appetite and pushed her plate angrily away from her. "I can't live like this. Do you want to be with me?"

"Of course I do. I wouldn't still be here otherwise," she answered eventually while rolling her eyes to the ceiling impatiently.

"Then you want to work this thing out?"

"What thing?"

"Don't tell me you haven't noticed," he said with a bite of sarcasm that Jessica took as a warning. The probability of him asking her to leave was slim but nevertheless had to be taken into consideration.

"I'm sorry. Yeah let's talk." She spoke in a softer voice.

"Tonight!"

Was he testing her? He knew how much she wanted to go to the party. She needed to meet some new people, needed to flirt, needed to feel alive and out of the tomb that she felt Richard would have been happy to keep her in for the rest of her life.

"Have you forgotten about the party?" She was firm.

"No, but I think our relationship is more important, don't you?"

Her choice was between spending an evening telling lies to a man she despised about how much she needed him then having to sleep with him to consummate them, and going to a flash party full of exciting new people! She wasn't bending.

"I am going to this party Richard."

She waited. And waited.

"Can we leave early then?" he asked.

"Of course we can," she said, offering a small morsel from her victory.

"See you later then."

"Bye."

"Jess?"

"Mm?"

"I love you."

He waited.

She hesitated.

"You too. Bye."

Jessica replaced the receiver then picked it up again to slam it down.

"Prick," she muttered.

Not long after Jessica had wandered upstairs, the bedroom became strewn with discarded clothes and fashion accessories. Jessica sat in the midst of the jumble-sale carnage and threw any article within reach across the room angrily.

What did it matter what she wore? It wouldn't make any difference. Richard would still wear something stupid and cling to her arm all night anyway. She wouldn't be able to make any kind of an impression with him beside her. He would negate all her efforts.

Feeling depressed and lonely she threw herself on to the bed and phoned Chris.

"Hello?"

"Chris, it's me."

"Jessica, hi. What's up?"

"I'm bored. Please come out to play."

"It's raining."

"I'll make you lunch."

"Is that a persuasion or a threat?" Jessica laughed. "I'm supposed to be going to see a film."

"I know but because your best friend needs you, you're going to go tomorrow instead. You're a wonderful man Chris, see you in about an hour?"

Chris laughed. "You are so bossy."

"You don't understand, I've got nothing to wear and it's the party tonight."

"Oh my God. Okay, see you in a bit for burned beans on charcoal then."

"No lunch at all for that," she scolded and put the phone down.

Jessica lay on the sofa and watched afternoon TV to block out the world until Chris arrived.

When he did, he came laden with bread, cheese and fruit, and dripping wet from the rain which still sleeted down behind him as he stood on the doorstep grinning widely.

"I thought it would be better all round if I made lunch," he said and blinked away the water that trickled from his hair into his eyes. Jessica thought it made him look quite attractive. Not that he was unattractive usually, but Jessica only sometimes noticed.

She gave him an extra special twinkle and dragged him upstairs. While he towel-rubbed his hair dry, she stripped down to her underwear. The very pretty underwear she had put on especially for him.

She tried on several outfits and showed them to him explaining the merits and pitfalls of each one, making sure she took plenty of time to stand in her pretty underwear between outfits.

"I think you look gorgeous in all of them," he said bending over his crossed legs.

"You're a great help, cheers."

She frowned at the scatter of garments over the floor then slumped on to the bed beside Chris.

"Okay, wear the dress, the dress looks stunning."

"The dress makes my arse look big," she sulked.

"Okay, the pants and shirt. They're smart."

"Yeah, for a job interview."

"Wear your jeans then." Chris laughed at her. He thought he might eat her if she sat there much longer.

"But they might all go smart and I'll feel scruffy," she whined.

She had already decided to wear the dress but she was enjoying sitting around in her underwear.

"Which do you like the best?" she asked.

"You looked especially beautiful in the dress." He really thought she did and painfully regretted that it was Richard taking her and not him.

"What about my fat arse?" she said and stood with her back to him so he could see it.

"You've got a wonderful arse and you know it," he said trying not to gawp.

Jessica smiled, she could always rely on Chris. "Fine, the dress it is."

"Does that mean we can eat now?" Chris scoffed and wondered how he was going to get out of the door without her seeing his erection. "I'll go and get it started," he said and hopped quickly down the stairs and tried to focus his mind on lunch rather than crippling images of Jessica in her underwear.

Jessica had smiled in triumph as she had watched him scurry from the room. It was very important that he fancied her because otherwise she couldn't have been his friend.

They ate and flirted and talked about Jessica because that was all they ever talked about. She didn't need to know anything about Chris other than what he thought about her.

Jessica looked at her watch.

"You'd better go before Richard gets back?"

Richard was jealous of her relationship with Chris. He couldn't understand why she had to have a friend who was male. He thought that he should be able to give her everything she needed from men.

"Okay but if you shag any stars tonight I want all the details."

He always wanted to know the details. He would listen hungrily, painfully swallowing each word with all the ease of gulping ground-glass.

"Perve," she laughed, kissed his cheek, squeezed his arse and closed the door behind him.

parties

The front door banged shut and Richard's voice called up the stairs.

"Are you up there Jess?"

"Yes," she shouted back reluctantly and quickly pulled on her dressing gown. She didn't want him to see her naked.

He walked in and put his arms around her waist.

"I'm sorry about this morning Jess. Forgive me?" He sounded cheerful which surprised her.

"Forgive you for what?" She liked it when Richard apologised. Just as long as he knew he was in the wrong.

"For being a whinging bastard on the phone."

He was trying to sweeten her so that she'd be nice to him at the party, so that they would appear a happy couple. She dodged the kiss that he was about to plant. "You'll smudge me."

Richard played a CD loudly to 'get them in the party mood'. Jessica sang along, happy that she'd been excused from having to talk to him and tried to forget altogether that he was there as she dressed and rehearsed various party poses in the wardrobe mirror.

She saw Richard pulling a suit jacket over a pair of jeans and her heart sank. She watched him as he danced a jerky jig to the music and wondered what she had ever seen to admire in him.

How could Jessica admit that what she'd admired about him and all the men before him alike, was simply that they could possibly love her? She preferred to think that she was just a bad judge of character. That she made mistakes.

"Ready darling?" Richard asked, still jigging. Jessica wanted to make him promise that he wouldn't dance or ask for autographs or cling to her or be boring or refer to her as 'his girlfriend' or talk to her or anything else that he might do to humiliate her. But that was asking for a different man. She sighed. That was exactly what she wanted.

*

The party was on the first floor. They could hear the music as they climbed the stairs.

Jessica walked ahead of Richard. She felt good in her little black dress. She thought she looked like somebody but Richard looked like the nobody he was and somebody might assume because she was with him that she was a nobody too.

She gained a few more feet on him but he quickly caught up and was standing by her side when the door was opened and Jessica found herself face to bosom with a woman whose beauty staggered her.

Jessica's confidence shrank slightly but not visibly. How short and fat she suddenly felt at the foot of this tall, thin column of soft, tanned flesh. The face of which, with its strong perfectly formed features was grinning down at her through a sheer curtain of straight, waist length white hair.

The smile was oddly distant as though she wasn't actually seeing them. Jessica decided it was the inane smile of a bimbo and immediately felt superior. She held her chin high at the long blonde beauty and flashed a patronising smile as she waltzed past her confidently.

"She looked like a fucking cardboard cut-out," she muttered to Richard whose eyes were yet to leave the sight.

"Will you buy me one for my birthday?"

Jessica flashed her eyes dangerously at him and began to walk away. It was typical that Richard would be taken in by a mindless tart.

It was a busy party and every square foot seemed to be spoken for. It wasn't easy to find somewhere to leave your boyfriend while you explore.

"Why don't you go and take our coats upstairs. I'll wait for you by the bar?" she said as she handed him her jacket.

"Don't you want to come with me?" Richard said doubtfully.

"I'd rather find a drink," she insisted.

"So would I."

"For fucks sake," she muttered just loud enough for him to hear and turned into the crowd angrily. He was following her.

Jessica was glad she'd worn her dress. She felt she blended well, which was more than she could say for Richard who shuffled uncomfortably in her wake, clutching her jacket against him as if it might provide some protection.

There were more beautiful people in that room than Jessica thought she had ever seen in her life and she was thrilled to be among them. She belonged there. She knew she did.

"Jess, wait."

She speeded up her step.

As she squeezed through the chatting, dancing crowds of beautiful people her eyes darted from one face to the next looking for one she recognised, or one that might smile at her approvingly. She planted a slight frown on her face to give the impression she was looking for someone specific and not celebrity searching at all.

The rooms were huge and well decorated. The white walls displayed gargantuan black and white stills of naked women in split beaver poses. Jessica wanted to stare at one. The sight of a ten inch cunt excited her but, not wanting to appear impressed, she strolled on.

She looked over her shoulder and caught a glimpse of Richard staring with his nose a few inches from the large cunt.

Jessica cringed and took advantage of the opportunity to lose him. She changed direction sharply.

Jessica picked up a glass of champagne from a tray and sipped it as she watched the party from the side-lines. She was disappointed that she hadn't seen anyone she recognised. She would've loved to have fucked a star. Or even chatted to one. Even to have been at the same party would have been enough. They were probably producers and directors, Jessica assumed.

Her eyes flickered over to the cardboard cut-out bimbo who was dancing outrageously in the centre of the room with a whole crowd of adoring men. Jessica looked on with envy and loathing. Men were so stupid, she though with disgust as they swarmed around the dancing beauty. Didn't they know how pathetic they looked? Couldn't they see that she was just playing with them, making fools of them? But even Jessica had to watch as the tall, elegant woman swirled and laughed confidently on her stage. Jessica quietly wished that she was her.

Jessica drank another two glasses of champagne and was just about to move on when a man brushed past her arm, spilling her drink a little.

"Sorry," he said, grinned, and hurried away. Jessica hadn't minded. She thought him stunning with his black hair and blue eyes. She tried to trace him in the crowd. Then she saw him. She should've known, she thought as she saw him dancing close to the beauty. She tried not to squint to get a clearer picture. She didn't want it to appear obvious that she was staring, but she was sure he was feeling her up under her dress.

Tart, she thought jealously and watched them as they left the room and disappeared up the stairs, followed by a small crowd of fashionable people.

Without them, the party seemed dull and lifeless to Jessica. The soul of it had gone upstairs. She wanted to be wherever they were. After a quick look around to check on Richard's progress, she moved smoothly toward the staircase and ascended.

She passed a couple of open doors upstairs. One room held a few men thrashing on electric guitars and a couple of girls, laughing and shaking tambourines in no apparent time. Another was a poky smoke filled room where people were lying around, rolling joints and not doing much of anything. Jessica, pretending to be looking for the bathroom, opened the last door wide and walked confidently in.

It was them.

She found herself under a spotlight of questioning eyes, which seemed to ask, "Yes?"

Jessica swallowed, suddenly feeling stupid.

"Sorry I was looking for the bathroom." She didn't want to leave but there didn't seem to be any reasonable excuse to stay and was just about to back out of the room when she saw what she had disturbed them from. The dressing table around which they hovered had a small pile of white powder on its glass surface. 'Drugs,' Jessica thought, a little shocked and excited.

"The bathroom's the next door on the left," someone said.

"Thanks," said Jessica, disappointed that they hadn't invited her in. Desperate action was required.

"Is there some of that going?" she heard her voice say. It was a risk, but she could always leave the party if they said no.

"Sure, come in and close the door." It was the dark haired man with the blue eyes that had nudged her arm earlier. She smiled at him, relieved at the welcome. But then as she turned her back on the group to close the door, her relief turned to dread and dropped heavily into her stomach. She'd snorted speed once when she was much younger and it had made her ill. Since then she had avoided drugs, which hadn't been difficult because she never came across them.

She watched as the man she recognised, chopped the small crystals expertly with a razor blade on the glass table. She hoped she didn't look as nervous as she felt as she watched him separate a small pile and shuffle it into a thick line.

"I didn't wet you before did I?"

He remembered her. She smiled demurely.

"Not with the drink."

"There you go," he said and smiled at her. For a moment Jessica was so taken by his smile that she forgot about her nervousness.

"Or would you prefer it in two?" She most certainly would, but she didn't want to be seen as an amateur.

"No, I like to take it in one. It's better that way," she said and hoped she sounded professional. He grinned and she felt pleased.

"After my own heart," he said and gave her a lingering look which sent Jessica soaring.

"It's excellent stuff," he added. From the appearance of his pupils Jessica guessed that he was talking from experience. She hoped her eyes would look like that. Wild and sexy.

He rolled a ten pound note into a tube and handed it to her.

"It's my turn now." Jessica looked over her shoulder to see the bimbo towering over her.

"Hang on Sophie. Go on sweetheart." He nodded Jessica toward the line which seemed to have grown since the last time she'd looked at it.

She wished everyone wasn't looking at her. She hoped her nasal passages were clear and she wasn't about to make ugly noises. And as she looked down the tube and at the powdery trail, she wished he hadn't been quite so generous.

She had to do this as though she did it every day of her life if she were to create the right impression. She leaned over the table and her hair swung down almost sending the lot over the floor. She stood just in time.

"Fuck, that always happens." She blushed furiously.

"Here." The man gently scraped her hair back from her neck and held it for her while she dipped her head once more towards what now looked like a small avalanche.

There was a part of her that wanted to say that she'd changed her mind and to run away, but the feeling of this man standing so close made that part very small indeed. She blocked one nostril and inserted the rolled note into the other. She ran the tube dextrously along the line watching in amazement how quickly the dust disappeared into it. She ran out of puff half-way and so exchanged nostrils, exhaled, and repeated the process.

She stood up straight and sniffed, rubbing her nose. She smiled at the man who was looking at her for her reaction. She wasn't sure how she was supposed to react. She felt nothing. Maybe it took time.

"Smooth," she said hopefully.

"Now will you cut me one?" It was the bimbo again.

He licked his finger and wiped up what dust was left of Jessica's line. Then he pushed his finger gently between Jessica's lips and wiped it around her gums. She thought she'd just discovered an unexplored erogenous zone.

It had pleased Jessica that he had made the bimbo wait until she'd finished. She sat back down on the bed and tried to swallow the vile taste that saturated the back of her mouth.

She watched as Sophie swiftly cleared two lines, both of which had been bigger than the one she'd been given.

"Better now?" he asked as she wiped her nose on the back of her hand carelessly. She kissed his mouth and squeezed her hand over his balls which gave Jessica a small stab of jealousy.

Sophie disappeared and he came and sat on the bed next to Jessica.

"I'm Jon," he said.

"Jessica," she replied and smiled just as she began to feel the first flush of the powder. First in her face, then her chest, throat and finally exploding in her head.

"Shit," she said as she felt a powerful warmth shoot through to her legs and cunt.

"Isn't it!" Jon laughed at her face. Jessica wasn't sure she liked it. Her hands were shaking and her heart was racing, pounding against her chest.

"I think I need to dance," she said standing up shakily hoping her worry wasn't apparent.

"Let's go."

Jon took her hand and they skipped down the stairs together. Jessica had forgotten all about Richard now. All she knew now was that she was "on drugs", that she felt brilliant, and that she intended to do anything it took to fuck this man who held her hand so tightly.

As Jessica danced, all her inhibitions floated away. She felt beautiful, sexy, confident. She loved everyone and everyone loved her. She felt wild, free. She threw her arms in the air and gyrated her hips to the music, pointing her cunt at Jon and staring into his eyes suggestively. Jon stared back and reached his hand under her dress.

Jessica didn't care who saw as Jon slipped his fingers under her knickers and pushed a finger up inside her. She was happy, exhilarated and horny.

Jon removed his finger and offered it to Jessica to lick. She sucked it and put her hand on his cock.

Jessica had never felt so good.

Then Sophie slipped between them. She was dancing, smiling, laughing. She took Jessica's hands and began dancing with her. They copied each other's movements, taking turns to lead, laughing wildly while Jon watched, laughing too as he danced beside them.

Sophie pulled her top off and flung it into the air so she was topless and shimmied her breasts at Jessica. Jessica – not to be outdone – slipped the straps of her own dress from her shoulders and pulled it down to her hips.

Both women swirled and laughed and danced and kissed Jon, kissed each other and each other's breasts. Just as Jessica was mid-swirl she felt herself being caught round the waist by somebody. It was Richard.

"Come on, we're going home," he said and began to pull her dress back over her breasts.

"What are you doing? I'm not going home. I'm having a great time. You go if you're bored but I'm not going anywhere." She pulled her dress back down like a petulant child and carried on dancing.

"Everyone's looking at you – you're making a total fool of yourself.

"No Richard, everyone's looking at you trying to make a fool out of me." Jessica was getting angry, which was sobering her up, which made her angrier.

"What's up?"

It was Jon.

"Nothing," she said referring to Richard. "Nothing at all."

Richard turned and walked away.

"Can I get some more stuff?" Jessica said into Jon's ear. She didn't want to say "coke" just in case it wasn't coke. Jon grinned and nodded for her to follow him. Jessica pulled her dress back on before she slipped her hand into his and walked with him back up the stairs.

Halfway up the staircase she looked down across the room and saw Richard sitting on a sofa staring up at her. She ignored him.

Jessica sat on the bed with all the coats while Jon retrieved an envelope from his pocket.

"Who was that guy?" he asked.

"It's the guy I live with I'm sorry to say."

"Is he always that heavy?"

"No, usually he's just pathetic."

"Why don't you get rid of him?"

"I already have. He just doesn't know it yet."

Jessica grinned up at him. She liked the fact that he was so interested in her business.

"You know the best way to do this don't you?" Jon said, standing over her with his fingers dabbing inside the envelope. Jessica didn't know but from the look in his eye she thought she might like it.

"Remind me."

"Take your knickers off," he commanded and while Jessica obeyed she thought she saw something pass across his face that she didn't like, a smarmy grin. She ignored it. It wasn't consistent with who she wanted him to be.

"Open your legs," he said. She did, although she would have preferred him to have asked nicely. He knelt in front of her and took his white dusted finger and pushed it up inside her which made her gasp. She did like it. Then he pushed his tongue first in the envelope and then on to her clitoris where he licked and tickled until Jessica felt herself go completely numb.

What had she been doing with her life until then, she wondered as she felt her spirits soar again.

Then he lifted her dress off completely and pulled her on to the bed with him where he kissed her.

Jessica was overwhelmed with the drugs, her passion but above all the new life she saw ahead of her. She had pulled the best looking man at the party. He had wanted her. He had chosen her.

Just then the door opened and Sophie walked in followed by two men.

"Oooh, can we watch?" said one of the men with a camp inflection.

"Disgusting," said the other with a grin. Jessica waited for Sophie's reaction.

"Don't be boring, come and dance with me," Sophie said.

"We're not bored, are we Jessica?" Jon laughed. Jessica wasn't sure what to say.

Sophie picked up Jessica's dress from the floor.

"You'll come and dance with me won't you." Sophie gave her a smile that made Jessica want to kiss her. Sophie liked her too. Everyone liked her. These were the type of people she belonged with. Jessica thought they were brilliant. She'd finally found some like-minded friends.

She stood up and allowed Sophie to dress her. Sophie rolled her dress down over her hips and kissed her on the lips lightly.

"You're very beautiful," she said and Jessica flushed with pride.

"So are you."

"I found her first," Jessica heard Jon's voice call as they left the room. It was wonderful to be wanted.

As she walked down the stairs with Sophie, Jessica couldn't see any sign of Richard. She hoped he'd gone home. She'd still have to face him tomorrow and there would be a scene of course, but Jessica wasn't going to let that spoil her fun now. For Jessica, now was all that there was.

Jessica had been introduced to lots of people that night. She had been kissed by most of them, chatted to a few and felt adored by all of them. She had been invited to other parties, been handed cards and phone numbers. Jessica thought she'd found heaven but nowhere more than when she was in Jon's arms. She found him charming, handsome, funny, popular and sexy. Most importantly, he made her feel she was all of those things too. With him she was the woman she'd always wanted to be.

It was light outside and most people had left the party. Jessica didn't want it to end, not ever. She was Cinderella. When Jon asked her if she wanted to go back to Sophie's flat with them, she jumped at the chance.

After saying good-bye to the host and the few remaining stragglers and being told how wonderful it had been for them to meet her and how much they looked forward to seeing her around, they stepped out on to the street.

Jessica's ears were buzzing and her stomach felt peculiar, like jelly. She guessed she was probably tired though the chance of her eyes closing in sleep seemed very unlikely as the drugs still had her lids pinned back.

She followed Sophie to her car, which was a brand new, red MR2. Jessica wondered what Sophie did to be able to afford a car like that. She was impressed and thought she might mention something about herself having owned a previous model years before.

"I'm off my head," Sophie announced as she slumped into the driver's seat. Jessica wasn't worried. She was busy trying to find a comfortable position on Jon's knee in the passenger seat.

"So what's new?" Jon said and pushed his hand between Jessica's legs making her jump and hit her head on the roof. They both collapsed in giggles and Jessica fell out of the car on to the road.

"It's a good job you're not driving," Jon said, pulling her back in.

Sophie drove far too fast through the quiet, dawn streets, with the music far too loud. And Jessica liked it.

*

In the kitchen of Sophie's luxury apartment, the three of them sat drinking whisky and eating bananas. Jessica found eating very difficult but Jon had assured her it would stop her "jelly belly" so she'd nibbled a little and decided to go with the jelly belly instead.

"You look exhausted," Sophie said with a mouthful of banana.

"I am," Jessica replied, wondering how Sophie could possibly swallow the mushy fruit.

"Come on, I'll give you a massage. It'll make you feel better." Sophie squeezed the back of her neck gently.

"Mmm, feels good." Jessica murmured.

"Let's play 'Sophie Says'," she heard Jon say. Sophie laughed and said, "Okay. Clear the table Jon."

Jessica watched curiously as Jon followed the instruction. What game was this? She thought they had a great sense of fun.

"Stand up Jessica." Sophie's voice was firm and Jessica stood, smiling, feeling in the spirit of the game.

Then Sophie pulled the straps of Jessica's dress over her shoulders and down her arms, pulling the dress with them so that her breasts were bared. Jessica began to feel a little nervous. The atmosphere had changed.

Sophie sat down on Jessica's seat, leaving Jessica feeling a little uneasy standing there in the middle of the floor, alone and semi-naked.

"Take it off," Sophie ordered.

Jessica hesitated. She looked to Jon for reassurance.

"Go on," he egged with a grin. The same smarmy grin she'd seen earlier.

The confidence she'd enjoyed earlier had now worn off with the effects of the drug and Jessica felt embarrassed.

She stumbled awkwardly as she lifted a foot free from the dress and blushed. But she felt she had to maintain her dignity. It would protect her. They could look at her body but they mustn't see her fear.

Jessica freed her other foot and stood slowly upright, now totally naked.

She had to do something to escape the unbearable silence.

She turned to face Jon. The desire she saw in his expression gave her the confidence she needed. Men's desire was something Jessica knew about. Familiar territory.

She walked as gracefully as she could past Sophie and sat on his lap, her legs astride his. She smiled at him and pressed her bare crotch against the rough fabric that covered his. The hardness she felt there encouraged her.

She lifted his face up to hers to be kissed but Jon didn't kiss her. He turned his head away from her.

Sophie laughed and Jessica froze.

"Sophie didn't say," Jon laughed.

Jessica was horrified. She didn't know what to do, but Sophie did.

"Come here sweetie. Don't be embarrassed." Sophie took Jessica's arm and helped her off Jon's knee.

More than anything else at that moment Jessica was furious with Sophie for highlighting her blush. She wanted to punch her, swear at her, punish her for it but instead she allowed her to push her against the table and kiss her breasts, throat and shoulders. Nor did she resist when Sophie laid her down over it on her back or when she pulled her thighs apart.

Perhaps Jon got off on watching, Jessica mused and felt a little throb of excitement in spite of herself. She would give him such a good show that he would be bursting to fuck her whether Sophie wanted him to or not.

"Has anyone ever tied you up Jessica?" Sophie asked.

Jessica found her head nodding. She couldn't let them know they hadn't.

"May we?" Sophie asked.

Jessica swallowed a nervous gulp. She felt she had to comply. She was angry with herself for being so weak, allowing Sophie to intimidate her into doing something she didn't want to.

"Please feel free," she said, smiling up at Sophie.

Sophie left the room for a few moments and returned with a handful of purpose made, leather straps. This obviously wasn't their first time. Jessica gulped nervously.

As Jon was binding her last free limb to the table leg, Jessica thought how similar this all was to her own fantasies.

She closed her eyes and tried to concentrate on the sensation of being tied.

Jessica jumped a little as she felt her face being covered. It was a mask. The smell of it reminded Jessica of the rubber swimming cap she'd worn as a child.

"Can you breathe okay?" Sophie asked, and without waiting for a reply, pulled the laces tighter round the back of her head.

It occurred to her with horror that they might hurt her.

"Don't hurt me." Jessica said.

"Were not going to hurt you, don't worry," she heard Sophie say with a hint of amusement in her voice.

Her back was aching already and she could feel pins and needles starting in her left foot. Jessica felt ridiculous.

That would never happen in her fantasies.

Jessica strained to listen for any sounds that might give her a clue as to what they were doing. No one was touching her and she couldn't feel them close to her. She heard the fridge door open and close and the rustle of cellophane.

She heard the sound of a buckle being undone and a zip then another rustle. Jon was undoing his trousers. A thrill shot through her body. He was going to fuck her.

"Stand there," she heard Sophie command.

Her body tensed as she felt the bare skin of what she assumed were Jon's hips between her thighs. Her breathing shallowed and her stomach tightened. Sophie was going to order him to fuck her.

Jessica pictured the scene and she could feel her vagina opening and closing, winking like an eye in expectation of Jon's cock.

She felt him lean over her. She prepared herself, drew in a deep breath, pulled against her restraints. Then Jon fell on top of her heavily forcing all the air out of her lungs.

Had he slipped? No, he was staying there, laying his whole weight against her. She could feel his cock pressed into her belly. Then he lurched forward, gasped and began moaning loudly into Jessica's ear, rocking back and forth on Jessica's body, grinding her spine into the table, painfully.

She struggled beneath him.

"You're hurting me."

Nobody seemed to hear her.

Jon's breathing was loud and irregular and the rocking became more and more violent. His cock was sliding up and down her belly making her wonder if he was wanking himself against her stomach. But where was Sophie?

Jon lifted himself a little and he took hold of both her breasts tightly. Sometimes his cock would poke her cunt or arse sharply but why wasn't he putting it inside her?

Jessica felt frustrated, angry and confused. He was pushing against her so hard that the table moved, making short scraping noises against the terracotta kitchen floor.

Jessica's feet had gone completely dead and her shoulder blades felt bruised. She wanted to shout for them to stop. She'd just have to hope that whatever they were doing wouldn't go on for much longer.

There was a cry of pain as she felt her breasts being squeezed by Jon's fists. Then a louder one from Jon as he shot his cum over her belly in short hot spurts.

He fell on her once more, breathless. Jessica didn't mind the weight this time. She was just relieved it was all over.

Jon and Sophie burst spontaneously into laughter and Jessica feeling outside the joke from beneath her blindfold had an urgent need to be dressed and decent.

"Get this thing off my head will you," she said in a light voice as though she was sharing in their amusement.

It was Sophie who unlaced and peeled back Jessica's mask. The bright light directly above her head stung her eyes.

Sophie was smiling down at her. She had half a cucumber in her hand. It was shit stained.

"Are you all right?" she asked.

Jessica wasn't really all right at all but she wasn't going to let Sophie know that. She looked at the cucumber again.

"Don't worry, you don't have to eat it," Sophie laughed and threw it into the bin.

"You're really special Jessica. I hope we can be friends." Jon smiled and hugged her warmly to him.

"Thanks. I'd like that." Jessica would've done it all over again just to hear him say that.

spaghetti

By the time Jessica arrived back at Richard's house, it was six o'clock in the morning. She was too tired to be anxious about what Richard might have to say to her. Too exhausted to care.

She stepped out of the taxi.

"Just give me a minute to get some money," she said to the driver who nodded patiently.

Jessica rang the door bell. She hadn't taken any keys.

It took a while for Richard to answer. She rang the bell a few more times impatiently. She needed to be in bed.

The door opened and Richard's squinting face appeared through the crack. He had been sleeping.

"Jess. What time is it?"

"I don't know. Have you got any money to pay this taxi?" she said and walked straight past, up the stairs to bed leaving him to deal with the driver.

She slipped off her shoes and dress, noticed she'd lost her knickers, and snuggled down beneath the quilt with a smile on her lips. Jon had really liked her. She could tell.

"Christ, it's six o'clock Jess. Where have you been?"

"At the party."

"Till now?" Richard sounded dubious.

"Yep."

"How are you feeling?" Richard's voice was tender and soft. Not at all what Jessica had been expecting. She was suspicious.

"Tired."

"I was worried about you. I shouldn't have left you there."

Jessica was on the very edge of sleep.

Richard climbed on to the bed beside her and stroked her head.

"We'll talk later darling. I just wanted you to know that I'm sorry," he whispered but Jessica was already asleep.

*

To her surprise it was dark when Jessica awoke. She'd slept all day. She fumbled for the clock and tried to focus her eyes on the digits. She was relieved to discover it was only six o'clock. She had arranged to meet Jon that night. She had two hours.

She heard a dull throbbing bass rhythm from downstairs that reminded her that she had to find a way of getting out of the house without Richard knowing where she was going.

She showered and decided to use Chris as her excuse. Though she thought she'd better give him a ring to inform him in case Richard phoned him to check up on her. She carried the phone into the bathroom and locked the door.

The answering machine recorded her message, which ended: "I'll tell you all about it in juicy detail. Cheers Chris. Bye."

She replaced the receiver and sighed. All she had to do now was tell Richard. She threw on some leggings and a sweatshirt and made her way downstairs.

The smell of something cooking wafted up the stairway and made her feel weak with hunger. She went straight into the kitchen to find Richard adding the finishing touches to a table set for two with flowers and candles.

Jessica was put on her guard.

"Hello darling, sleep well? Sit down and I'll get you a drink. It'll be ready soon."

Jessica said nothing as Richard kissed her lightly and led her into a chair. She wanted to know what was going on. Why wasn't he angry with her?

"What's all this in honour of?" she asked quietly.

"More will be revealed later," he said. If he had something to say why didn't he just tell her?

Richard brought her drink and sat down opposite her.

She eyed him over the rim of her wine glass and recognised a certain childish glint of excitement. He was up to something and it made her nervous.

Richard put his glass down and took a breath.

"I want to apologise for last night."

Jessica didn't know what to say. She was staggered.

"Sometimes I depend on you too much. You're confident in crowds but I just go to pieces. I felt so small in that room. I wanted to hide behind you and I was angry with you because you didn't want me to. It was only when I got home that I realised I had no right to blame you. It must be like having a little kid clinging to your skirts all the time."

"Forget it. It's over now." Jessica was wondering how she was going to escape.

"You've got to let me make it up to you." Jessica saw the glint again.

"Really Richard it's okay."

She wished he'd quit while she was ahead.

"You see I get jealous. Not of other people but of you."

"Smells nice."

"Spag Bol. I'm proud of you, you see. I want people to know that you're my girlfriend. I feel great when you're with me." Richard was becoming more and more earnest. Jessica went to taste the Bolognese sauce.

"That's nice. This looks great. Shall I put the broccoli on to steam?"

How could she get away?

"Not yet, the spaghetti will take ten minutes. Jess, what I'm trying to say is that I think we're worth working for."

Jessica was filling a glass of water from the tap with her back to him, rolling her eyes impatiently.

"Jess."

"Uh huh?"

"Will you sit down, please?"

Jessica complied. He extended his arm across the table and held his hand open for Jessica's. She resisted the sigh and complied again. He was looking at her with a certain intensity that made her feel uncomfortable. She couldn't keep his stare so she let her gaze fall to where her hand lay limply in his. Richard squeezed it. She looked at him. He was smiling at her softly. Then he pulled something from the back pocket of his jeans that filled her with dread.

He placed it on the table in front of her.

"Marry me Jess."

Jessica could only stare in disbelief as he showed her the ring.

"I've never wanted anything more," he added. Jessica couldn't bring herself to look at his face. Why hadn't she seen this coming?

"Say something," he laughed nervously. Jessica glanced up at him briefly.

"I'm speechless." She was meeting Jon in one hour and wasn't even dressed yet. Why did he have to do this to her tonight?

"You only have to say 'yes'," he said quietly.

Jessica hated hurting people. She wanted to meet Jon. She didn't want a scene. She wanted to keep everyone happy. But she *was* going to meet Jon. She could say "yes" for now and then break it off later. But then he wouldn't want her to go out. And she had to go out. If she said "no" there would be talking. It would be the end of the relationship. She would have to leave him. It was his house. Where would she go?

"Yes." There, she'd said it.

Richard sighed in relief. "For a moment there, I thought you were going to say 'no'."

"How could I when you asked so beautifully." Jessica forced a tender smile and walked around the table to sit on his knee. He held her tightly and buried his face into her shoulder. She cradled his head while he wept and told her how happy she'd made him. She stroked him and wondered how she was going to announce her imminent departure.

"Come on. Let's eat. I'm fainting with hunger." Jessica climbed off him and served their dinner.

They ate in silence.

Until she said, "Shit."

"What?"

"I was supposed to meet Chris tonight."

"I'm sure he'll understand." Richard smiled in the way one might expect a man to who'd just got engaged. "Why don't you give him a ring and tell him our news?"

"Okay."

Jessica walked through to the lounge, leaving the kitchen door wide open. She pretended to dial a number and waited. Then she had a conversation with herself.

"Hi Sue, it's Jessica here. Has Chris left yet? . . . Shit! I'm not going to be able to make it . . . Oh no, you're joking . . . Jesus Christ. How was he when he left? . . . Listen if he phones tell him I'm on my way . . . Yeah . . . okay. 'Bye."

"What was all that about?" Richard asked with a frown.

"That was Sue, his girlfriend," she said and sat down heavily at the table as though she'd had a shock.

"And?"

"Apparently, Chris's mum died this morning. She said he left in an awful state, to meet me." Jessica hoped she sounded convincingly worried.

"How did she die?"

"I didn't ask. I'll have to go to him Richard," she said seriously.

"Jess, no." Richard whined, shocked that she could even suggest leaving him on their special night.

"Richard, he's my friend. I can't abandon him now. He needs me," she pleaded.

"I'm going to be your husband. I need you," he insisted.

"How could you be so utterly selfish?" Jessica said.

"Me selfish?" he guffawed.

Jessica was really annoyed. She had afforded him more humanity than this.

"I'm going Richard," she said firmly and finally. She rose from the table and went upstairs. As quickly as she could, she grabbed her catsuit, boots and make-up and stuffed them into a bag. She could change in a cafe toilet.

"When are you going to wake up Jess?" It was Richard. Had he seen her from the door?

"What do you mean?" she asked, genuinely confused.

He walked in and sat on the bed. Then he looked at her, his expression pained but strangely calm.

"You don't want to marry me," he told her. "Do you?" Jessica looked down at her feet.

Silent foot staring.

"Do you?" His tone demanded a reply.

"No," she said.

"No," said Richard. "I didn't think so."

"I'm sorry Richard." And she was.

"Yeah, me too." He got up and walked to the door.

"Let me know when you want to collect the rest of your stuff."

There was moment of panic for Jessica. Where was she going to go? Should she talk him round? Of course that would mean not going out. No, Jessica thought she would rather be homeless than not meet Jon. Besides Chris would let her stay with him for a while, if she had to. Jon might even put her up. The latter possibility decided her.

"Will you be all right?" Her voice was soft. She was sorry she'd hurt him. Really sorry.

"I'll have to be won't I." She heard the bitterness in his voice and just for a moment, felt his pain. The pain she'd caused. And she hated herself for it. So much so that she almost rushed to him and begged forgiveness and a second chance.

But Jon was waiting. Her new life was waiting for her.

Jessica added a few more things to the few already packed and walked slowly down the stairs.

Richard was sitting in the lounge staring at nothing in particular. Jessica hovered in the doorway.

"I'd better be going," she said.

Richard looked over his shoulder at her. She could see he'd been crying.

"Is this it then?" Jessica cringed at his cliché and avoided his eyes.

"I think so," she said quietly and wished he would just let her go but he continued to hold her there with his stare.

"I really love you Jess."

"I know."

He looked back into his nothingness.

"Take care Richard."

She turned her back and as she opened the front door she heard his sobs. She knew they were his final plea. He wanted her to rush back but she was already gone.

She closed the door quietly behind her and ran down the cold, dark street in case he should call her back.

sleeping over

Jessica felt nervous as she entered the bar where she'd agreed to meet Jon. She felt stupid in her tight catsuit and wished she'd worn something a little less sexy.

What if he wasn't there? She'd look stupid then. Then she saw him. Her disappointment at finding him with a large group of people instead of alone was diluted by the sheer relief of him being there at all.

She made her way over towards the loud, boisterous crowd. She recognised one or two men from the party. She smiled as they looked her over.

They made space for her around the table eagerly.

"Jessica, great you made it." Jon beamed at her. "We're going to a club. Coming?"

"Absolutely." She was going wherever he was.

"Let's go then." Jon stood and everyone else took his lead. Jessica decided they had been waiting for her.

"Where's Sophie tonight?" Jessica asked him casually as they stepped on to the street.

"She's meeting us at the club." Jon replied.

"Oh good," she lied.

"Hey Jessica, your catsuit's giving me a hard on," someone said behind her. She turned and laughed appreciatively. She liked it.

"He's not the only one," Jon said, which she liked more.

"Hey Jon," another voice called. "How about letting Jessica come in our cab?"

"In your dreams Ben boy," Jon shouted back, laughing at his friends. He put his arm tightly around Jessica's waist and kissed her neck. "She's all mine."

Jessica had been transported to some place of ecstasy.

She was all his.

They approached the line of black hackney cabs and began to fill two. Just as Jessica was about to climb into the second, Jon pulled her back.

"Let's take one of our own," he said.

She liked this a lot.

He came and sat beside her on the seat.

"You look incredible," he said hungrily when they were alone

"Thank you," she laughed and thought the same of him.

"You can see the shape of your cunt in that you know."

Jessica blushed. "Can you?"

"Look." He traced the outline of her vagina with his finger. Jessica held her breath as she watched him.

"How did it go with the boyfriend?"

"Ex-boyfriend," she corrected. "I left him."

"Good," he said and Jessica soared higher still.

"Do you want to do a speedball?"

More drugs, Jessica assumed.

"Are you going to do one?" she asked.

"I've done one."

"In that case, I'd love one."

She watched as Jon took a small clear plastic bag from his pocket. It was half filled with a fawn coloured powder. Not balls at all Jessica noted.

"One condition," he said.

"What?"

"You have to take it from the end of my cock," he laughed.

"What about him?" she nodded towards the driver.

"He won't see and if he does it'll give him something to wank about later."

"Whatever you say," she laughed back. Whatever he said.

Jon freed his penis which Jessica was pleased to see was already erect. She took it as flattery.

Jessica usually avoided oral sex with men. She didn't like it. But she wouldn't have done anything to disappoint him. So she watched while he sprinkled a small heap onto the tip of his penis. She bent her head and dabbed it with her tongue until it was gone. She screwed up her face against the bitter taste, then sucked him into her mouth and bobbed her head up and down on his cock, until the taxi pulled up outside the club.

"Christ Jessica, you know your stuff," he flattered her again.

Jessica smiled. "Practice," she said, feeling sick.

It wasn't until they had met up with the others and Sophie that Jessica began to feel the effects of the 'speedball'. It wasn't the same feeling as she'd had at the party. It was gentler, more subtle. It seemed to be slowing down her movements, making her feel sensual and erotic.

She looked over at Jon who had excused himself saying that he had to talk with a friend. He stood at the bar with two middle-aged men wearing suits and ties. They seemed most unlikely friends for a man like Jon to have. But Jessica was more focused on herself to think about it too much. She had begun to feel nauseous.

"Are you okay Jessica?" Sophie seemed concerned as she looked at Jessica's colourless face.

"I think I'm going to be sick," Jessica said quietly.

"Has Jon been feeding you speedballs?" she asked knowingly. Jessica nodded.

"He always make them too smacky. Come on. You'll feel great once you've thrown up." Sophie led Jessica through the club to the toilets. Jessica had to run the last few yards and still only made it to a hand basin.

Sophie handed her a paper towel.

"Feel better?"

"Yes. That was almost a pleasant experience," Jessica laughed. Sophie had been right. She did feel wonderful.

"What did you mean by 'smacky'?"

"Smack. He mixes too much heroin into the coke."

Jessica's face fell. Heroin. She had taken heroin. She looked in the mirror at her eyes. Her pupils were tiny but after a moment's hesitation, Jessica decided she felt too good to care what it was and tidied her hair and face.

They walked back into the club.

"The show's starting." Sophie said.

Jessica looked to where Sophie pointed. There was a girl on the stage. It was a strip show. Jessica tried to look blasé. But it was difficult. She wanted to stare. She wanted to stand close and stare, open mouthed.

Sophie took her hand and led her to where the rest of their group were standing, close to the stage, just where she wanted to be.

"Jess, Sophie, over here." It was Jon shouting them over.

"This one's great," he said excitedly over the music. He put his arm around Jessica's shoulders. She liked that.

Jessica watched as the woman danced. She was threatening to remove her knickers, waving her arse in their faces. Jessica watched the men around her jeering and cajoling each other, shouting suggestions to the naked dancer who ignored them. Jessica was thrilled.

The atmosphere in the audience was one of hysteria as everyone shouted and laughed and cheered. It wasn't how Jessica used to imagine they'd be at all. She'd thought it would be all men wanking beneath macs under tables. But as she looked around her there were groups of women, young and older, couples, young men, and fashionable types like the group she was with.

So Jessica yelled and stared as comfortably as everyone else. The woman removed her knickers right at the end to rapturous applause, then bowed away from the audience giving them all a quick glimpse between her buttocks before she made her exit.

"She was brilliant," Jessica said to Jon, like an expert.

"Yeah but this is the best bit," he said nodding to the stage as the MC called for another round of applause for the woman who'd just finished.

He called for hush and announced that it was time for the 'open spot'. Jessica looked round excitedly as he called for "any ladies who'd like to have a go." There was much jostling and shouting of names but no one seemed to be stepping forward.

"Go on Jessica," Jon urged.

"Bollocks," Jessica laughed.

"Why not? You'd be brilliant." For a moment Jessica thought he was serious.

"Go on. It's a good rush. I've done it," said Sophie.

They were serious.

The rest of their group chimed in.

"Come on Jess. It'll be a laugh."

"For you maybe," she scoffed. Unfortunately for Jessica, they seemed to take her quip as an affirmative response and began to call the MC over.

She had been enjoying the attention up until then, but now she was panic stricken.

"Ladies and Gentlemen. We have a taker," the MC shouted into his microphone and Jessica was dismayed to see he was looking at her.

There was loud applause as Jessica found herself being hoisted on to the stage by her 'friends'.

"What's your name sweetheart?"

Jessica found a microphone in front of her face but lost the ability speak.

"Jessica!" her 'friends' shouted.

She turned and saw Jon grinning up at her. Then she saw Sophie and decided that if she could do it, then so could she. She looked bravely into the audience and blew a kiss at them, which was received by cheers and shouts. Jessica didn't know if it was the drugs or her adrenalin but she felt as though she were flying.

Jon would be impressed. The audience would love her, want her. It was enough.

"Ladies and Gents, Jessicaaa." The lights went down and the music came up. Jessica was shaking all over but it felt good to be up there with everyone looking at her. She felt powerful and the drugs softened the edge of her fear.

Her eyes closed involuntarily as they had been doing on and off since she'd been sick. She allowed them to stay closed as she began to dance. She was dancing for Jon. She imagined it was just him and her.

She pulled the zip of her catsuit down exposing her back and shoulders. She could hear them cheering her on. Encouraged, she pulled her arms free and rolled it to her waist. Then danced some more with her breasts bared. The cheers got louder. Jessica couldn't stop herself from smiling. They liked her. So she liked it.

She hooked her thumbs into the garment around her hips and began to slide it down a little further until it was just above her pubis.

She laughed as she heard their shouts of encouragement and turned her back on them to inch the material over her bottom. She gave them a couple of seconds then pulled a brief moony at them, bowing deeply like the girl before her had done. Then she pulled it back up, waved and ran for Jon at the edge of the stage.

Everyone was clapping, cheering. She was a star.

Jon lifted her down and hugged her warmly.

"Fucking brilliant," he laughed.

"Nice one Jessica," Ben said.

"Excellent," said one of the others.

"I hate all of you," she laughed. They all congratulated her, kissed her, slapped her on the back.

Flushed, flattered and excited, she was the toast of the evening.

The MC called for another round of applause for "Jessicaaa". She couldn't help smiling.

Jessica had a wonderful time for the rest of the night. People she didn't know came up to her to offer her their impressions of her performance. There were free drinks coming from her ears and Jessica considered stripping for a career.

*

It was late by the time the trio arrived at Sophie's flat. Jessica eyed the kitchen table dubiously, but she needn't have been worried.

"To bed I think," said Sophie. "Coming?"

Jessica was relieved that it had been taken for granted by the couple that she would be staying with them. She would have hated to have had to ask.

The bedroom was huge and completely empty but for a vast bed in the centre of the room.

"Room enough for three?" Sophie laughed at Jessica's open mouth.

"Room enough for thirty," Jessica said and had a childish impulse to jump and roll on it.

"We've never tried thirty, have we Jon?" Sophie said with a conspiratorial smile that made Jessica suspicious. She didn't like the way that Sophie referred to herself and Jon as 'we'. She thought that Sophie did it on purpose to exclude her.

Still, what did it matter, she thought as she caught Jon's eye winking at her. She had her own 'we' developing.

Sophie began to undress where she stood and Jon sat on the edge of the bed and did the same. Jessica suddenly felt a flush of bashfulness for which she felt ridiculous, considering.

She shook the feeling off and stripped quickly not wanting to be the last undressed and in bed.

Sophie unscrewed the top from a pill bottle and tipped a couple of green egg-shaped capsules into her hand.

"Want some sleepers?" She offered her hand out to Jon.

"Not tonight," he shook his head. Then she looked at Jessica.

"No thanks, I'm almost asleep now." Jessica laughed. If Jon didn't need them then neither did she. Sophie shrugged her shoulders and swallowed the green eggs.

Jessica wasn't sure whether there was a certain protocol to

be followed or what was expected of her. Jon climbed into the bed first and waved her over. He pulled back the quilt and she slipped in beside him, closely followed by Sophie. Jessica was in the middle.

Sophie reached over her to switch off the spotlights attached to the centre of the headboard. Her breasts brushed against Jessica's shoulder and made her shiver. Jessica thought they were magnificent, much fuller than her own with huge red nipples.

Sophie resumed her position and all three lay still and quiet and naked in the darkness.

"Glad you came?" Jon asked quietly.

"Yes," Jessica whispered back.

"Me too," said Jon.

Jessica wanted so much to roll over and kiss him, to thank him. She would've liked him to have rolled on top of her and pushed her thighs apart. At that moment wanting sex had little to do with desire and more to do with a need for reassurance. She was single now. And alone.

Jessica, lying on her back, could feel Sophie's breath. It was steady and rhythmic. Jon's too sounded shallow. And yet when Jessica tried to close her eyes, they bounced back open, spring-loaded. She had too much to think about to sleep.

She put her arms behind her head and let her thoughts flicker over the events of the evening. She thought of Richard. He would be alone and heart-broken, crying into his pillow. But that was his choice, she thought harshly as she felt a twinge of guilt and put the thought firmly out of her mind. She had other concerns now. She turned her head towards Jon.

"Not sleepy?" he whispered.

"No." She was glad he was awake.

"Want some help relaxing?"

"What have you got in mind?"

She felt Jon's hand slide across her thigh to her cunt in reply.

"Mmm." She squeezed her buttocks together to lift herself slightly from the bed. She lifted a leg over his hip to offer him better access.

Jon was wanking her gently and Jessica was trying to keep her breathing under control lest she should wake Sophie. She didn't want Sophie to join in. But it was difficult, and Sophie was disturbed.

"If you two are going to mess about, do it on the floor quietly. You're making the bed jiggle." Sophie sounded slightly angry but only at having been disturbed from her sleep. Jessica couldn't figure out what the connection was between her sleeping hostess and Jon. They were obviously sleeping together and yet her presence seemed to be totally accepted.

Jon climbed out of the bed and signalled for Jessica to follow him. He led her down the stairs and into the lounge. He switched on the lamp. He knelt on the rug and pulled her down in front of him.

For once Jessica didn't feel the need to take over the leading role. He made her feel safe for some reason.

He laid her down on her back, stroked the hair from her face lovingly and smiled at her. Jessica felt her eyes soften as she smiled back.

She was excited and happy. Jessica thought she might have met somebody very special.

He kissed his way down her body taking pauses to look at her while Jessica lay still and watched his gradual descent. He opened her thighs and lay between them with his face so close to her cunt that she could feel his breath warm against it.

She rested her head on the floor and closed her eyes, preparing herself for Jon's tongue but first she felt his fingers stroking her lightly, dipping inside her a little then sliding gently all around the folds of sensitive, swollen skin that lay nestled between her labia.

He pressed his lips against them firmly and licked her with the tip of his tongue. Jessica lay perfectly still and for once her thoughts remained with the sensations that Jon was creating in her body. She felt no pressure to do anything but lie there and after a while something very unusual happened. Jessica came.

She felt it growing, snowballing from deep inside her. It surpassed any orgasm she had ever given herself. She thought she might explode as it continued growing until it finally reached its climax and her body flooded with a calming warmth.

Jessica had never cum by a man's efforts alone before and a tear flowed out of her eye in celebration.

He laid himself on top of her, supporting himself on his elbows so he didn't crush her beneath his weight. He was thoughtful. He licked the tear stain from her temple and kissed the eye from which it escaped.

There was silence as they lay staring into each other's eyes. Jessica suddenly had no doubts. She could see a tenderness in his eyes that she thought she knew and now she wanted to love him. She thought at that moment she perhaps already did.

They crept back into bed gently next to the sleeping Sophie.

"Thanks," Jon whispered softly and kissed her mouth.

"What for?"

"For being here." He kissed her again.

Jessica was happier now than she'd ever been. She slid her arm under his head. He snuggled in closer to her and nestled his face into her neck. He rested his hand on her breast and gave it a little squeeze.

Jessica stroked his back lightly with her fingers and before long Jon was sleeping in her arms.

He was her prize.

He was everything she had ever wanted. And he wanted her.

Jessica slept well that night. Her future was dawning on the horizon.

sleeping over

The challenge of a new man might seem an insignificant goal in life to some but to Jessica it was the only thing worth working for.

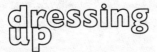
dressing up

Jessica awoke to the sounds of Jon and Sophie moving around the room. She opened one eye a little and saw that they were dressing. Shutting it again quickly she pretended to be deep in sleep, hoping that they wouldn't disturb her. Jessica didn't look her best first thing in the morning.

She strained to decipher muffled words from whispered tones. Were they talking about her?

The bedroom door was opened and closed but it wasn't until she heard the front door bang shut and the sound of a car pulling away that Jessica felt safe enough to sit up.

She looked around the room, slightly dazed at how she came to be there. Twenty-four hours ago she stepped out of one life and into another, which wasn't especially unusual for Jessica. She'd done it lots of times before but with considerably less risk than she felt she'd taken this time.

For the first time, she felt some doubt. Should she go back and patch things up with Richard? She despised him but at least she knew him, knew where she was with him.

No, she thought as the image of Jon formed in her mind. She had made the right decision. Jon really liked her. His friends liked her. She had a good time with them. She took drugs and stripped in nightclubs.

Jessica put her hands over her face in shock as she remembered her performance at the club. Had she really done that?

She went into the bathroom.

On the basin, she saw an envelope lodged behind a tap with her name on the front. She opened it nervously.

Inside was a note from Sophie folded around a fifty pound note.

It read, "Hope you slept well. Help yourself to clothes, you should find something to fit you in my wardrobe. I've left you some cash in case you need any. Jon'll be home about four."

It was just signed," Sophie."

Jessica thought again what nice people they were. She was a relative stranger and yet they had opened up their home to her.

She was grateful.

She began to fill the bath-tub with hot water and the bathroom with steam while she explored a little.

There was a door at the far end of the bedroom behind which Jessica discovered Sophie's wardrobe.

Her mouth fell open as she stepped inside. It was wall to wall mirrors. Even the tiled floor was so highly polished she could see her reflection in it.

She slid back the mirrored closet doors one after the other to reveal the largest collection of designer wear she'd ever seen. There were shelves of shoes and boots, belts, bags, scarves and hats. Jessica felt as though she'd just walked into an exclusive Italian fashion house.

Thrilled, like a little girl with free rein in a sweet shop, she began to try them on, parading up and down the room like a model on a catwalk. She thought she looked great in them and when Jessica looked great she felt great; confident, arrogant, superior. She wanted to go out in them and show the world how wonderful she looked.

She would go and see Chris. She needed someone to show off to.

"Shit!" she cursed suddenly remembering the filling bath. She fled into the bathroom in time to catch the water beginning to spill over the edge of the tub. She turned off the taps, pulled the plug and mopped the water from the floor with a towel.

Once she was satisfied that any evidence of near disaster had been cleared away she climbed into the semi-circular tub and submerged herself into the soothing hot water.

Just at that moment Jessica felt deliriously happy. She'd fallen on her feet again and now all she had to do was make sure she stayed on them. She patted herself on her back for her achievement. She was a survivor all right. She always got what she wanted.

Things were going well for Jessica. She was back in control and there was nothing more satisfying than that.

Comfortable and contented, Jessica slipped her hand between her thighs and pushed a finger inside herself.

Bath-tubs were one of her favourite places for wanking, especially when it was someone else's bath-tub.

She opened her legs wide, crooking one knee over the side of the bath and closed her eyes.

She saw herself naked in a large cage. There were men all the way around it and some had climbed on top. They were all reaching their arms through the bars trying to touch her but the cage was just big enough so that if she stayed in the middle they couldn't reach her.

She was teasing them.

It was a show.

She rubbed her breasts at them, lay on the floor for them and spread for them. She wanked herself off at them. She wanted them to see the full glory of what they'd never have; what she would never let them have.

They were groaning in unison, begging her to let them have her. She was laughing at them and she was cumming.

It was a good strong orgasm and being alone she was free to let it out vocally. A deep, throaty growl escaped her and resonated loudly in the acoustics of the bathroom.

Jessica lay limp for a few minutes, her hand resting over her cunt, and resolved she would use that fantasy again.

Jessica dried and pampered herself with Sophie's expensive lotions and perfumes and nosed leisurely through all the cabinets and drawers.

There were the usual potions and first aid sundries but the

cabinets mainly housed dozens of small brown pill bottles. Someone was a hypochondriac, she thought. She also found a tube of haemorrhoid cream, which made her smile. Sophie had piles.

Jessica spent the next hour or so swanning around the luxurious apartment naked – making sure she posed whenever she passed a window in case there should be somebody watching. Jessica liked the idea and hoped someone was.

This was the sort of place she should live in, Jessica told herself as she fingered the quality upholstery of the suite.

She selected a Patty Smith CD from the hundreds on the shelf and played it loudly, dancing in the sun-flooded lounge room. She ate grapefruit at the breakfast bar in the kitchen, lay full-length on the sofa and watched TV on the huge hi-tech screen. Then she lay on her stomach with her legs splayed on the thick-piled carpet in a shaft of sunlight that bathed her backside and she phoned Chris.

The phone rang and rang.

"Please be in Chris," she pleaded into the receiver. She wanted to tell someone of all the exciting changes taking place in her life and she had no one else to tell. She wanted to show off and Chris was always a good candidate for that because he was always impressed.

Finally he answered.

"Hello?" His voice was groggy with sleep. Jessica had woken him up.

"Get up. It's a beautiful day and I want you to meet me," Jessica said brightly.

"Is it? What time is it?" he said through a yawn.

"I don't know. Afternoon probably, you slob," she said affectionately.

"I was working till four."

"Pathetic excuse. How long will it take you to get to Soho?"

"Hang on, let me think."

"There's no time for that, I've got loads to tell you. I've left Richard," she said excitedly.

"What? When?"

"That woke you up," she laughed.

"Where are you now?"

"No, that's it. If you want to know any more, you'll have to meet me."

There was no doubt he would.

"Jesus Jessica. Okay. At the cafe?"

He knew she knew he would. There was no question of it.

"Where else! See you there in about an hour then. Bye darling."

She put the phone down and ran upstairs. She hadn't decided yet on which of Sophie's outfits she would wear.

She selected a pair of black leather trousers, a long-sleeved white leotard and a pair of crocodile skin boots which she had loved from the moment she saw them.

She applied some mascara and red lipstick from the collection of make-up in the bathroom, tied her hair back tightly and borrowed Sophie's Ray-Bans which, unlike hers, were actually Ray-Bans.

Checking herself out in the hall of mirrors she thought she could easily pass for one of the rich society brats that she envied so much.

Jessica adapted to her new persona very well. She looked and felt the part as she walked down the street to look for a tube station. It was only then that she realised she didn't know where she was.

She stopped a well-dressed man in his fifties.

"Excuse me. Could you tell me how to get to the tube station?" Jessica said in an accent befitting someone of her new status.

"Which one would you like?" he asked in a similar accent to the one Jessica was faking.

"The nearest please," she said, not wanting to admit that she didn't know where she was.

"Let me see, I don't use them very often."

"Me neither, the car's in for a service," Jessica cut in hurriedly.

"Richmond station is the nearest but it'll take you a good fifteen minutes if you're walking. Why don't I give you a lift. My car's just in the next street," he said and smiled at her innocently.

Jessica hesitated for a fraction of a second before accepting.

"That's awfully kind of you, thank you. I shall be terribly late otherwise," she said gracefully and wondered if she'd overdone the accent a bit.

"It's quite all right. It's more or less on my way."

Jessica followed him as he crossed the road and walked on to the street he'd indicated. He turned into the drive of an enormous house that she tried to look unimpressed by.

"Just give me a min. She's in the garage." He disappeared through a door leaving Jessica alone in his driveway.

She thought he seemed genuine enough but that didn't stop her being prepared for him to make a pass at her, or grope her. Men were men no matter what age or class and she trusted him as much as she did any of them.

The garage door slid up on its electric roller and out pulled a brand new white BMW. Jessica nearly squealed in delight.

She was impressed by wealth.

She wondered if she'd be able to persuade him to drive her all the way into Soho. On the other hand there would be more people to see her in her new outfit if she took the tube. She weighed the options as she settled herself in the large comfortable passenger seat and reached for the seat belt.

"Here, allow me to help you." Aye aye, Jessica thought. We haven't even got out of the drive.

He reached his body over her and pulled the belt towards him. It fell across her right breast and when he inserted it he pulled it tight so that it squashed her flat. She freed herself as subtly as she could – with no doubt that he'd done it on purpose.

"There we are," he smiled and Jessica smiled back sweetly. They were off.

Jessica thought he was driving painstakingly slowly and she was becoming aware of the time. It must surely be an hour since she had spoken to Chris and she wasn't even on the tube.

"Are you meeting a boyfriend?" he enquired politely but Jessica knew where that question was leading.

"No, my publisher," she lied calmly.

"But you do have a boyfriend?"

"Yes, that's who I live with," she said firmly.

"What do you write?" he said showing a polite interest.

Jessica loved being given the opportunity to talk about herself and she was glad he'd dropped her sex-life from the conversation.

"Plays mostly," she replied.

"Really. How wonderful and what sort of plays do you write."

"All sorts. I get commissioned to produce scripts around various themes. My latest is touring the North at the moment but it'll be in London early next year." Jessica was starting to really enjoy herself.

"Oh really? What's it called?" Jessica thought he sounded impressed.

"Sophie." She answered confidently.

"I shall keep my eyes open for it."

"Thank you. I hope you enjoy it."

Jessica felt very tall indeed.

"I don't suppose you'd like to go for a coffee?" he asked after a short silence.

Coffee my arse. "Thank you, no. I'm already late."

He pulled the car into the kerb in front of the station.

"Well here we are. It was lovely to meet you," he said grinning at her tits and offered his hand. "I hope I see you around sometime."

I bet you do, she thought. "Yes," she said. "Thanks ever so much for the lift."

"Good luck with your writing."

"Thanks. 'Bye."

Jessica slammed the car door and gave a little wave as he drove away. "Dirty old git," she said through her smile.

She walked under the arch into the station, lifting her glasses on to her head. She hated people who wore sunglasses inside. She couldn't abide posers.

She made the journey standing and her ego swelled a little more with every glance she received. Taking each one from men as approval and lust and from women as envy and respect.

By the time Jessica reached the cafe in Soho she was bursting with confidence. She looked great and everyone had noticed.

As she approached the cafe she saw Chris sitting at one of the tables outside.

Once again, he struck her as being quite handsome.

"Darling. Thank you for coming." She kissed his cheek and sat down beside him.

"You said an hour," he frowned at her.

"I know, I'm sorry but that was before I remembered that I didn't even know where I was. It took ages to get here." She pouted and sparkled at him and he laughed.

He found it impossible to remain cross with her and, besides, he was just relieved that she'd phoned him at all. He thought she must still have been angry with him after the last time they met. But Jessica had forgotten all about that.

"What do you mean you didn't know where you were?"

"Well, I've met someone I really like." Her eyes sparkled.

Chris's heart sank.

"Who is it?" He did his best to sound interested.

"I met him at that party the night before last. Oh Chris you wouldn't believe what's happened in the last couple of days."

"Tell me." He found himself smiling at her excitement in spite of his pain.

"We got to the party and Richard was being a dickhead as usual so I wandered off. You should have seen this house. It was huge and there were pictures of cunts everywhere. Amazing. Anyway, this guy started to chat me up, we did some coke and I ended up dancing topless."

"Typical," Chris interrupted.

"What's that supposed to mean?"

"Typical exhibitionist behaviour. What happened then?" Chris said encouraging her. He loved to see her sparkle like this. It made her look all the more beautiful to him.

"Richard got all possessive and started to try and take me home. I told him I didn't want to go and he hit me in the middle of the dance floor." Jessica had hardly stopped for breath, revelling in her version.

"He did what?" Chris flushed in anger which was exactly what Jessica had wanted him to do.

"It's all right, I threw a bottle at his head," she laughed and Chris took his cue, as he always did, to laugh also.

"Nice one Jessica," he cheered.

"Then he walked out," she concluded.

"What was everyone else doing while all this was going on?"

"They just stood there, gobsmacked. They were really nice actually. Especially Jon. I think he could see I was pretty upset so he offered me a place to stay." Jessica's eyes were shining. Chris knew there was more.

"So you went back to his place?"

"Yes. He wants me to stay with him for a while. Oh Chris, I really like him." Chris swallowed.

"So what happened with Richard?"

"I didn't get back to the house until late morning, slept all day, and when I woke up there was a cosy meal for two laid out and he asked me to fucking marry him. Work that one out."

"Easy. He didn't want to lose you." Chris understood how that felt.

"He should have thought about that a long time ago," she said bitterly, losing her sparkle for a moment.

"What are you going to do now?" he asked.

"Enjoy my freedom," she replied and sparkled again.

Chris smiled. He was happy that she was happy but he was devastated. There had always been that little spark of hope in the back of his mind that when she finally left Richard it would be for him.

Jessica sensed his sadness and felt a little guilty. But she had had to tell someone. That's what friends were for.

"Come on let's go for a walk," she said. There were still hundreds of people out there who hadn't seen her outfit yet.

Chris put a few coins on the table and they left.

Jessica put her arm around his waist so he put his around her shoulders. She squeezed him and looked up at his face. She wanted to reassure him that he was still important to her.

"There's nobody I'd rather spend a sunny afternoon in Soho with," she said. Apart from Jon that was. He squeezed her back affectionately and they strolled toward the market.

It never occurred to Jessica that the same stalls might work different markets and so when Chris stopped to look at a pair of jeans, the last thing she expected was to see a familiar face.

A familiar large face with a familiarly large mouth.

"What happened to Wednesday," the mouth said and Jessica's stomach turned over.

Chris turned round and Jessica looked at him. She was sick with panic. She had to get out of there. She didn't want Chris to know what she had done.

The mouth saw her glance and drew his own conclusions.

"Oh I see, this your boyfriend is it?" He looked straight at Chris and winked at him. "Nice cunt that one, tight." he said to Chris and licked his large lips.

It was obvious to Chris that he was being challenged and his first concern was to get himself and Jessica away. He took her arm.

"Just keep walking," he said firmly and Jessica was glad he was there otherwise she might've had to let him fuck her again.

"Cheap too, only cost me a pair of jeans," he called after them as they walked away.

Jessica was crying behind her Ray-Ban's. She'd been caught out.

"I'm sorry about that Chris." She was trying to think up a story to explain what had happened but Chris didn't need an explanation.

"It doesn't matter Jess. He's gone. Come on, I'll buy you a cream bun." His gentleness touched her and she smiled at him, genuinely grateful for his tenderness though she didn't know how to tell him that. Jessica found it very difficult to accept any unconditional kindness. She always assumed there must be a hidden motive.

She was reminded of who she really was. She didn't know why she did the things she did; what it was that made her lie and hate; what it was that stopped her being able to love anyone or allow anyone to love her. It was the just the way she was. And she hated it.

Chris walked her back to the tube and listened while she fumed and raged about men who couldn't handle rejection from women. Men like the stall holder whose delicate male ego she had damaged.

He put his arm round her shoulders and said nothing. He knew she lied to him. He knew she wasn't all she pretended to be but he forgave her because he understood that all was not well with Jessica. He had always known it. She had proved herself a liar on more than one occasion. Once, he had half-challenged her about it. Her reaction had been sufficiently violent to warn him not to do it again.

He didn't hold it against her. There was nothing she could do that would change his opinion of her.

Jessica pecked his cheek and waved farewell without telling him about Sophie. That would have spoiled the story.

kissing

Jessica tried to time her return so that she would arrive back at Sophie's house a little after Jon. If she got there before him it would mean her waiting on the doorstep as she didn't have a key and, besides, she wanted him to think she'd had a busy day. At the same time she wanted maximum time alone with him. Sophie hadn't said what time she'd be home and so she may not have long.

The tube pulled in to Richmond at quarter to four which gave her twenty minutes to get home, five minutes after he did. Maybe she would walk slowly to give him ten, five might seem a little eager.

As she walked, asking various people directions to Sophie's street in various accents, Jessica thought about Richard.

She wondered whether he would try to contact her. There was still the matter of retrieving her belongings from his house. She wished she didn't have to face him at all and could close the door on the whole memory. She didn't want any bitterness. They were both mature adults and would resolve the issue with decorum, she thought doubtfully.

The MR2 was nowhere to be seen. Sophie wasn't home.

Jessica brushed her fingers through her hair, walked up the path and rang the doorbell.

She was nervous. Her stomach tight. Her mouth dry. She didn't know what to expect; how he'd be with her; whether he would acknowledge the night before; whether he would want her again. He opened the door widely and grinned down at her.

"Had a good day?" he asked, brightly.

Jessica almost felt coy.

"Not bad, busy. And you?" She walked past him into the hallway.

"Wonderful," he beamed, closed the door and spun round to face her.

He slipped his arms round her waist and kissed her full on her mouth.

Jessica felt elated. He still wanted her.

"I wanted to say thank you for last night." He was looking straight into her eyes.

"Any time."

"It would seem you owe me one," he said suggestively and pulled her in closer to him. She wished he wouldn't grin in that smarmy way. It spoiled him.

"It's only fair," she said and reached up to kiss him again.

Jessica thought he kissed her beautifully. He was tender and gentle but just demanding enough to make it exciting. He didn't slobber his spittle all over her face nor did he try to choke her on his tongue. He pressed his hands into the small of her back passionately instead of ramming them up between her legs like so many of his predecessors.

He was like the men in her fantasies. She could have created him. He was made for her. He belonged to her and she would have him.

She didn't broach the subject of Sophie or her expected time of arrival as Jon began to undress her there in the hall behind the front door. What did she care anyway when Jon was unbuttoning the front of her leotard? Slowly, carefully he pulled it down from her shoulders and over her wrists.

Kissing her breasts gently he knelt to undo the button and zip of Sophie's leather trousers, easing them over her hips and down her legs. Then he removed the boots.

"Lean on me," he said and she did, lifting one foot after the other so that he could take them off completely.

She stood naked and he knelt at her feet.

"You are so beautiful Jessica," he said in a breathless whisper as he looked over her body.

She liked the way he said her name. She liked the fact that she pleased him.

Once again he led her to the rug that lay in the centre of the lounge room floor. It was nice to be held by him. Nice to be kissed by him. Nice to be alone with him.

She lifted her leg over his hip as they lay on their sides, facing one another and directed his cock to the entrance of her vagina. She pushed her pelvis forward to receive him but to Jessica's horror, not only did he not push back but he quickly shrivelled until his stiff erection lay limp and flaccid in her hand.

This was not something Jessica was used to though it wasn't unknown. She thought she had done something wrong. She didn't turn him on. She shouldn't have taken the initiative. She knew from experience that some men didn't like it when women did that. It took away their masculinity. And she had so wanted to please him. She wanted him to want her again.

"With your hand" he said.

Jessica was disappointed. Why didn't he want to fuck her? What was wrong with her? She collected the penis that lay flaccidly against his thigh and began to massage it.

He lay very still while Jessica worked at building his erection. Once he was stiff, he shuffled on to his side away from her and nuzzled his arse against her belly.

What now? She wanted to be entered, plunged, loved, not play concubine.

"Finger my arse," he whispered over his shoulder.

Jessica wasn't enamoured by the idea but she wanted to do her best for him so she wetted her fingers anyway and rubbed them along the crack between his cheeks, circling his anus with her fingertips. She pushed a finger a little way inside him and felt his body stiffen so she pushed it all the way up as far as it would go and Jon brought his knees up a little further to his chest. She squirmed as she felt the shit high in his rectum. She drew back her finger and slipped another in beside it. Then she fucked him slowly with her two fingers while she reached round to his cock with the other hand. She drew back his foreskin while she pushed her fingers up deep inside him. She pulled and pushed her fingers and his foreskin simultaneously until she felt his cock erupt into her hand.

He lay still for a few seconds and Jessica smeared his semen over his chest and stomach. Then she pulled her fingers from his arse, careful to hold them away from herself. They were caked in his shit.

"Thanks," he said and rolled on top of her to kiss her. "I really like you being around."

"I like being around."

More kissing.

"We had better make ourselves decent before Sophie gets back," he said with an apologetic pout.

"Why? Would she mind?"

"No, but I don't want to rub her face in it."

Food for more confused thought. Did that mean she would be displeased? She hadn't seemed to have minded the night before.

Sophie had been nice to her, mostly. Jessica even quite liked her at times, but that didn't stop her from wishing that she didn't exist.

Jessica felt frustrated that their time alone together hadn't been longer.

"What time is she due?"

"In about five minutes." Jon laughed at her panicked expression and rolled off her.

"She could've been early," Jessica said.

Jon held out his hands and she took them for him to pull her up.

"Better dress quickly then."

He kissed her mouth and she skipped out into the hall, collected her clothes and took them up to the bathroom to wash and dress.

As she scrubbed the shit from beneath her fingernails, she

enjoyed feeling happier and lighter than she could ever remember.

She grinned at her reflection in the mirror.

"Happy now?"

And Jessica was happy. She was giddy with happiness. It didn't matter what anyone did to her now. As long as she had Jon she didn't care about anything else. She even felt a little benevolence towards Richard. Only love could do that, she thought with a girlish laugh and went back downstairs.

Jon was making a pot of coffee in the kitchen. She stood behind him, put her arms around him and squeezed. She pressed her cheek into his shoulder blade and sighed as he reached his arm behind him to press her in closer.

Jessica wished she could freeze that frame and live in it for ever; create a harbour that the tide of time would miss so that Sophie would never come home. Jon would be beautiful with her always and she would remain young for him. They would be lovers for ever without complications and all the outside forces that destroy the ecstasy of fresh love.

Then there was the sound of a car door snapping shut. Jon patted her buttock as a signal that she should move away from him, which she did reluctantly.

Sophie breezed into the kitchen looking extremely elegant in a fitted suit and Jon greeted her with a kiss that burned into Jessica's stomach.

Sophie looked over his shoulder at her.

"Hi there. They suit you," she said referring to her clothes that Jessica was wearing.

"Thanks. I appreciate the loan," she said sweetly, hoping her loathing of Sophie, who was still standing in Jon's arms, wasn't apparent.

Jon went back to pouring the coffee while the two women sat at the large pine table.

"We seem to spend a lot of time in kitchens the three of us, don't we?" Sophie said with a grin and Jon laughed.

Jessica was mortified at the mention of her humiliating ordeal but rather than give that away, she laughed as loudly as Jon and Sophie, if not a little louder.

"So what do you do when you're not stripping in nightclubs?" Sophie asked pleasantly and they all laughed again at Jessica's expense.

She hated this question whenever it arose for what could she answer, sit in cafes, buy cheap imitation designer goods and shag the occasional stranger?

"I write plays for stage and radio," she said confidently.

"Really. Anything we might have seen?" Jessica felt flushed suddenly.

"I doubt it, most of my work was produced in the North. I havn't really written much while I've been in London. It's so much more difficult to discipline oneself here. There's too many distractions."

Sophie seemed to have lost interest in the subject and was now flicking through her diary. Jessica felt stupid for bothering to answer her question in the first place.

Jon came and joined them at the table.

"We're meeting some friends for a meal tonight. Would you like to come?"

Jessica had little else to do. She nodded. "I'd love to."

"Who is it?" Sophie asked him, almost sullenly Jessica thought.

"Roger and Annette," he replied chirpily.

"Oh."

Jessica noted the alteration in Sophie's mood. She didn't seem thrilled. Jessica wondered why. An uncomfortable silence seemed to have fallen and she didn't feel it her place to ask why?

Sophie stood and left the kitchen. Jon smiled reassuringly at Jessica before he followed her into the hall.

Jessica strained to hear their conversation but what she heard was broken and confusing. Sophie sounded angry and Jon seemed to be trying to calm her. Then she heard footsteps ascending the stairs and the kitchen door opened.

She tried to look as though she hadn't been listening as Jon walked back in.

Jon didn't acknowledge the upset so neither did she.

"If you go up, Sophie said she'd find you something to wear," he said without looking at her.

Jessica felt dismissed.

"Okay."

As Jessica entered the bedroom she saw Sophie bending over a magazine on the bed. She was snorting a line of white powder. She didn't seem to be aware of Jessica's presence. When she'd finished, she threw back her head and sniffed.

She saw Jessica and put her fingers to her lips.

"Ssh!" she said and slipped the magazine under the bed.

"Makes things easier," she added and wiped her nose on the back of her hand.

Makes what easier? Jessica wondered.

"Let's see what we can find for you." Jessica followed her into the mirrored closet room.

Sophie pulled out a few different outfits before selecting, without consulting Jessica, a pale gold-coloured dress.

"Try this on." Jessica undressed to her knickers and stepped into the dress. Sophie zipped her up then stood back from her to look.

"Oh no that's no good," she said with a frown and pulled the skirt up around Jessica's waist and began to pull Jessica's pants down. Feeling slightly alarmed, Jessica allowed her to pull them free of her feet.

"I'd forgotten this one's too sheer to wear anything under-neath," she said and pulled the skirt back down over Jessica's exposed pubis. "What do you think?"

Jessica thought that there was nothing about the dress that necessitated not wearing pants.

She checked out her reflection from every angle which was easily done in that room. She would've liked to have been allowed to choose her own outfit but, reluctant as she was to admit it, she probably would've chosen this one. She felt rich and beautiful in the short silk dress that flattered her every angle, fitting without clinging.

Ordinarily she'd have been thrilled moist by the idea of appearing in public in a short dress without knickers but because it was at Sophie's suggestion it only made her feel badgered, made her feel under orders.

"I love it. It's beautiful. Thanks Sophie."

"It suits you. Keep it," she said and without giving Jessica a chance to thank her she unzipped her and held it open for Jessica to step out of it leaving her naked once again.

"We'll find some shoes after we've showered."

Sophie took the dress and laid it on the bed and proceeded to take her own clothes off while Jessica was left to interpret the "we" in "we've showered."

She wandered into the bedroom after her. Once again she thought how incredible Sophie's body was and it made her want to hide her own.

Sophie collected Jessica's hand and led her into the bathroom. Jessica was getting used to being led. Sophie turned on the shower and stepped inside the tall glass box while Jessica waited silently for the next instruction, feeling stupid and awkward because she didn't know what to do or what was expected of her.

"Come on then," Sophie called. Jessica stepped inside and Sophie slid the door shut.

The tall glass box was filled with steam within seconds and Jessica could hardly make out Sophie's face.

"Not too hot for you is it? I like it boiling," Sophie called over the noise of the falling water.

"No it's fine. Is there some soap?"

"Here let me." Jessica felt Sophie's soapy hands slide over her shoulders and neck down to her breasts where she lingered far longer than was necessary to clean them. Jessica felt her nipples harden in Sophie's fingers, her body reacting in spite of the fact she didn't want it to.

Sophie stepped closer and smoothed her hands down over Jessica's buttocks, sliding her fingers between the crack.

"I'm always horny when I'm stoned," she said, grinning. Jessica thought she must therefore always be horny because it seemed to Jessica that Sophie was always stoned.

Sophie's breasts rested on top on Jessica's and their soaped skins touching felt smooth and soft.

Jessica wanted to touch her breasts. Sophie lifted Jessica's chin and, while the shower rained down, kissed her, so Jessica guessed it would be okay. She reached up and massaged them one at a time.

It was nice while it was like that, soft and tender but Sophie's kiss got harder and her squeezes more vigorous. Jessica felt herself being pushed against the glass and Sophie's knee forcing its way between her thighs. It stopped feeling nice. Then Sophie's fingers were inside her. Jessica didn't know how many but enough to be painful as she began to fuck her with them. Then she brought her other hand down behind her and pushed more fingers into her arse.

She would've liked to have told her to stop but it was too late for that. Jessica resigned herself to Sophie's physical demands.

Sophie's face pushed between her thighs. Jessica opened them to enable Sophie to suck her. It was best to get it over with as quickly as possible. After a short time, Jessica groaned and writhed alternately, before thrashing out a melodramatic orgasm.

To her horror Sophie didn't stop. With her face in her cunt and her fingers up her arse, Sophie only licked and pumped harder.

Jessica was confused. Had she not made it clear enough?

She peered down at where Sophie was kneeling and through the steam saw that she was wanking herself. Then it was clear. Sophie was there for herself, not for Jessica.

Just then Sophie sank her teeth into Jessica's fur, and released a deep roar that vibrated through Jessica's pubic bone.

Either not hearing or caring about Jessica's squeal of pain she continued biting until her orgasm was over.

"Mmmm nice," she said as she switched off the shower. "You've got a wonderful cunt." She kissed Jessica's cheek.

"We better hurry or Jon will be wondering what we're up to." Sophie handed Jessica a towel and began telling her how good the Chinese restaurant was, as though nothing had just passed between them.

Jessica found herself dazed again. And flattered. Sophie wanted her too?

"Are you nearly ready?" came a shout from the bottom of the stairs.

"Come up. We're done." Sophie called back, winking at Jessica and Jon was soon in the bathroom with them.

Jessica felt guilty when he smiled at her behind Sophie's back but she was used to guilt and had little problem masking it. She puckered her lips at him and winked.

Half an hour later, still sore from Sophie's bite, Jessica climbed on to Jon's knee in the passenger seat of Sophie's car, in nothing but Sophie's dress, with no idea of what lay ahead.

bathtime

When the trio arrived at the restaurant they were greeted by the manager who took their coats and escorted them to a table in the centre of the room.

Jon took Jessica's hand. "Come on I'll introduce you. You look amazing by the way," he added and smiled in a way that made her nerves subside. She didn't need to worry about anything when she was with Jon because he made her feel so good about herself.

She might have felt intimidated by the plush interior, the respectful waiter, the glitter and stench of hard cash that drifted from the surrounding tables, but Jessica took it all in her stride. She held her head high with the same arrogant disposition that she perceived around her, not allowing anything to pass across her face to say that this was anything less than she was used to.

As they got within Jessica's range of focus, she was surprised and disappointed to see that Roger and Annette were old and respectable. Not the sort of people Jessica had expected at all. They weren't a bit like Jon's other friends.

The large overweight man stood and beamed at Jessica as he held out his hand which she took politely.

"Well hello. Who is this beauty Jon?" Jessica forced a smile as he undressed her with his eyes.

"This is Jessica," Jon announced.

"Hello Jessica. I'm Roger and this is Annette, my wife," he said and his wife nodded her head and smiled.

"Hello," she said. "You're just in time. We were just about to have an almighty row which would've been frightfully boring. This will be much more fun." She directed this last sentiment at Jon and smiled at him as she took his arm. Jessica thought she detected that certain intimacy that is usually only found between lovers and felt instantly threatened.

Roger pulled Jessica's chair out for her, seating her between himself and Sophie, opposite Jon and Annette.

They were older than Jon and Sophie by about a decade which made them two decades older than Jessica. She felt very young and awkward and stupid in the little silk thing that she was wearing – that Sophie had given her to wear. The men were dressed in suits and the women sported shoulder pads beneath their designer silk jackets and slacks. Had Sophie dressed her like a little girl on purpose to make her look foolish? she wondered suspiciously.

The waiter poured them some wine and handed them each a leather-bound menu. The older couple ordered for everyone.

Jessica felt like sulking. She hadn't been allowed to choose her clothes or her food.

"Trust me," Roger leaned over to her as the waiter took away the menus. "You'll love it."

Jessica forced a smile and said nothing.

She hardly said a word the whole evening and sorely regretted being there at all. She had to sit and watch and say nothing as Annette flirted with Jon, pushing her cleavage out at him and grappling under the table while he laughed in mock protest.

Jessica was furiously jealous but laughed merrily at Roger's terrible puns and tried to look interested in the conversation he and Sophie were having across her. She couldn't understand what these two people had in common with her trendy new friends.

It wasn't until Sophie excused herself to go the ladies that Jessica felt she was required to give anything to the evening, though she would've liked it to have been something other than her thigh. Roger was brushing the palm of his hand against her leg while talking to Jon.

Jessica was dumbfounded.

This overweight, middle-aged man to whom she had hardly spoken a word was making his way up her dress and was just about to find out that she was knickerless.

What could she do? Nothing without making a scene and

Jessica wasn't one to make a scene. Holding her breath, waiting for Roger's imminent moment of discovery, she searched desperately for an escape that wouldn't incriminate or embarrass her.

"You're quiet Jessica. Are you okay?" Jon asked and as Jessica opened her mouth to reply she felt Roger's fingers against her pussy. She closed her mouth and nodded.

Annette whispered something into Jon's ear that made him laugh and once again they were wrapped in each other's attentions.

Jessica turned to look at Roger. He grinned a dirty grin and pulled his hand out from beneath her skirt and licked his fingers.

Jessica was shocked and disgusted. She wanted to empty her glass of wine over him, stand, call him something witty and demeaning in a loud voice and storm out of the restaurant with everyone looking after her in awe. They would all look at him in disgust then lower their voices to call him a filthy old rake.

Sophie returned seconds later. Feeling relieved and grateful, Jessica smiled warmly at her and Sophie reached over to squeeze her knee.

A friendly gesture, Jessica thought until the gentle squeezing became a firm tugging that was forcing her legs to open. Jessica wondered if she was starring in a pornographic farce and raised her eyes briefly to the ceiling to roll them in exasperation at the situation.

She was sure Roger would see Sophie's strategy. He'd have to be blind to miss it. She glanced down to see the tops of her thighs in full view and Sophie's outstretched arm moving right between them.

She pulled her skirt down a little, the tablecloth up a little and gave Sophie a warning glance but Sophie only smiled back reassuringly and pursed her lips as if to shush her and slid her hand all the way up to her crotch.

Jessica lowered her eyes in frustration only to raise them

again in shock as she felt Roger tugging at her other knee. Jessica panicked. He would find Sophie's hand already there.

It was too late to do anything about it and she bit her lip as she felt their two hands meet in the middle.

What would happen now?

Nothing happened.

She glanced at Sophie who smiled and winked. Jessica gulped back a tear of humiliation as they continued their conversation across her while sharing her pussy between them.

Sophie had probably planned it. Bitch, she thought, as she sat silently staring at the food for the sake of somewhere to look.

They were trying to make her cum opposite Jon and Annette, in a busy restaurant.

This was a very different world for Jessica indeed and while she didn't want to appear prudish – Jessica was game for a laugh – she just didn't think this was funny.

Why didn't Jessica just get up and walk out? Because Jessica belonged to anyone who wanted her.

She didn't know how to apply her right to refuse.

Having established that she couldn't stop them verbally, she decided to pull herself away physically. She pushed her chair back and while still sitting announced that she must excuse herself to the ladies room. Both hands recoiled to their owners and Jessica was free to stand and walk away.

Behind the locked cubicle door Jessica felt safe enough to put her head in her hands and sigh. What was she doing here with those sick people? Was he really worth it? she wondered. He'd better be, she thought, or he'll pay twice over for what she was having to go through in order to have him. And what about Sophie? What was she playing at? She was sure that it excited Sophie to see her humiliated.

Jessica didn't want to leave the safety of that small safe box where nobody could reach her or see her. The toilet was the only place Jessica felt she could justifiably be alone and sometimes she wished she never had to leave it.

But she couldn't afford to be too long or she might risk being questioned when she returned to the table.

She washed away their fingers with an all too familiar wad of damp toilet paper then quickly checked her reflection.

There were two vending machines on the wall behind her. She went to look just in case they were selling steel knickers with invincible crotches.

A deep breath and back to the front line.

"Ah, Jessica. I've just invited Jon and Sophie round to our house for drinks so you must come too or I shall be hurt and think you don't like me," Annette pouted pleadingly.

Jessica felt quite sick.

Like you ? I can't fucking abide you, Jessica thought. *Silly pompous stuck-up bitch.*

Jessica would've loved to have smeared the red from her crinkled, ageing lips across her stupid pouting face but instead she smiled sweetly and accepted the invitation. She had little choice if Jon and Sophie were going.

Roger paid the whole bill without comment and the waiter brought their coats.

"You go with Sophie and I'll go with Roger," Jon said. Jessica was disappointed. She liked sitting on Jon's knee.

Jessica's spirits were low as she sat in the passenger seat of Sophie's car which was following Roger's white Mercedes through London's night streets.

She gazed out of the window as they passed gangs of young people enjoying themselves and ached to be among them.

She saw a couple holding each other tightly as they strolled and considered whether it was odd that she should desire to be held like that?

She was feeling slightly abandoned by Jon. Maybe if she told him what Roger had done he'd be angry, protective of her. Jessica desperately needed protecting but she knew she was on her own. She couldn't rely on anybody to look after her, experience had taught her that.

Sophie was strangely silent as she drove.

"How long have you known Roger and Annette?" Jessica asked, curious as to how their friendship with such a couple developed.

"Only a few months," Sophie replied.

"Does he always feel up women when he first meets them?" Jessica asked, bitterly.

"Oh, he's only having a laugh." Sophie sounded irritated by her question, which made her feel stupid for mentioning it.

There was an awkward silence that Jessica couldn't bear.

"How did you meet them?" she said to break it.

"Jon does business with him sometimes."

Jessica suddenly realised that she didn't know what Jon did.

"What sort of business?" she enquired, chattily.

"All sorts," Sophie answered cagily.

"Oh." Jessica took the hint and asked no further questions.

Finally the cars turned into the driveway of a large house. Jessica wasn't surprised by their wealth. It exuded from their every pore. She had expected nothing less.

They were shown into a dark room. Only the corners were lit, by small orange spotlights. They seated themselves on two large sofas opposite one another with a glass coffee table between them and were brought heavy crystal glasses containing generous shots of expensive brandy.

Roger hit a button on the stereo and some classical music sounded loudly from hidden speakers. Jessica jumped. It was very loud, too loud for anyone to talk so nobody spoke.

Jessica stared into the glowing embers of the fire in the grate to avoid having to look at anyone. She felt embarrassed by the loud music that she didn't recognise and their consequent silence.

She was sitting on the same side as Jon and Annette which had been only a fractionally better alternative than sitting with Sophie and Roger.

She felt she needed to be near Jon even if that did mean being near Annette who was apparently glued to his side.

Glancing up for a second to where Roger and Sophie sat she was shocked to find them wrapped in each other's arms and kissing violently. Open-mouthed, she turned to look at their respective partners alongside her for their reactions.

Jon had his arm around Annette's shoulders and Annette had her hand inside Jon's flies, each totally engrossed in watching as Sophie and Roger were pulling at each other's clothes till they were naked.

Jessica felt invisible, as though she would be able to leave the room without anyone noticing, but she couldn't help being fascinated by the scene being played out in front of her. It even surpassed the feelings she might have had concerning Annette's hand on Jon's cock.

Jessica was quite stunned. This was a real life wife swapping party she was observing and she found it fairly amusing until she questioned where she would fit into it.

Would she be expected to take part?

Roger was now on his knees on the floor between Sophie's legs which were splayed over the arms of the sofa. Jessica was impressed noting that she was almost doing the splits.

There was something comical about Roger's big fat white whale-like body grovelling on the floor, lapping at Sophie's cunt, when she let him. And she couldn't help laughing when Sophie began smacking him hard across the face every time he licked her. Then she wrapped her thighs around his head and kicked her heels into his back.

Jessica was cringing with each thump. Surely he must have been in agony, she thought as Sophie rained a series of blows down on to his flabby back that made his loose flesh wobble.

On the contrary, Roger seemed to be enjoying the abuse very much.

Jessica shuddered. She hated pain on any level and sexually it just made her dry up instantly.

Feeling like a little girl, Jessica's eyes widened with wonder.

She had always liked to think of herself as sexually experienced, open-minded, uninhibited, but this was something new indeed.

She was so engrossed in the other couple's activities she didn't see how Annette's head came to be bobbing up and down on Jon's cock.

Then she began to feel stupid because she was alone. She didn't want to look but she could hardly pretend she hadn't noticed what was going on nor did she want to join in. Perhaps she might've if Jon had invited her to be with him.

She wanted to leave but didn't want Jon to know that she'd been shocked. He might think her a frigid virgin type and not be interested in her any longer.

With that in mind, she wondered if she should involve herself somehow. She couldn't just sit there and not do anything.

There was that nervous knot in her stomach again as she deliberated what her first move should be.

Annette sat up and removed her blouse and bra. Her breasts fell out of their supports and sagged like empty purses onto her ribs.

Jessica felt like laughing. Did this old drooping woman think she was any match for Jessica's firm youth? Sophie and Roger were now taking their turn to sit and watch the activities on the other sofa. They watched, as Jessica did, while Jon pushed a banana from the fruit bowl on the coffee table up the older woman's cunt.

Jessica felt out of place and uncomfortable as Annette masturbated while the banana fucked her. Jessica's embarrassment was almost causing her physical pain. She wished she could just vaporise, vanish. The feeling was doubled when Annette's screaming orgasm could be heard over the music.

Jon pulled the banana from her and replaced it into the fruit bowl. Jessica was just wondering what would happen next, when she suddenly became aware that all eyes were on her.

She was frightened.

She looked at Jon for support but he was wearing the slimy

grin, which made her feel distinctly alone. But, as he walked over to where she sat, it turned into a comforting smile. He held out his hands. She took them and allowed him to pull her to a standing position. He kissed her deeply. Jessica was stirred by the intensity of his kiss and decided that she wouldn't mind them watching, that it would be sexy. They would all see how much he wanted her. Sophie would envy his tenderness and the couple would envy her youth.

She relaxed and began to enjoy the idea.

Jon was lifting her dress. She raised her arms for him to remove it completely. Now she was naked and Jon was laying her down on the glass table top. She maintained his eye contact. She didn't want to catch anybody else's eye. He kissed her forehead and winked at her. Then he stepped back from her.

She frowned. Where was he going?

Then she felt her knees being opened. She looked down. It was Roger. He was preparing to enter her. Jessica put her head back and closed her eyes.

No, she shouted in her mind. She felt tricked, humiliated.

Seconds later, Annette sat astride her breasts. Her wet cunt was sticking to Jessica's skin and she was trying to wank off while her husband banged his flabby belly and minuscule penis against her groin.

She felt her head being turned to the side. She opened her eyes to see Jon on his knees with his cock in his hand. He pushed it into her mouth.

She could see Sophie, sitting on the sofa calmly sipping her drink, watching.

It was her body being crushed and pounded but she wasn't in it. She had projected herself to somewhere above the scene where she hovered, laughing bitterly. It stopped her from crying. So this was how the upper echelons of society spent their evenings.

Jon came and she let his semen dribble from her mouth. Annette licked it from her cheek, then stood over Jessica's face and wanked herself again. Her juices dripped on to Jessica's face and neck.

It was only Roger who hadn't yet cum. Jessica had had enough. She needed it all to be over. She pulled herself from Roger's clammy grasp and sat up. Then she took hold of his penis, and beat it with the little energy she had left, resolving not to stop until her arm dropped off or he came.

Eventually he did.

She sighed in relief. Her arm was shaking.

She stood and collecting her crumpled dress from the floor, she left the room to find a bathroom without looking at anyone.

She needed to cleanse herself of the mess and the memory.

Jessica lay in a deep steaming bath. The bathroom door was locked and she felt sick with exhaustion and disgust at herself and at them.

But mostly at them.

She pictured a still of the scenario around the coffee table and laughed through her tears at the farce.

"Welcome to bourgeois society, dahhhling!"

babysitting

Over the next few weeks Jessica was subjected to many new experiences by Sophie and Jon, their friends and various 'business associates'.

She wasn't unaware of the peculiarity of their behaviour. She knew it wasn't normal but then Jessica had never really experienced normality.

Jessica focused on what she understood to be their kindness and hospitality. They never asked her what her intentions were regarding her near future. They never challenged her about her financial dependence on them. They didn't seem to begrudge her anything. What had she to complain about?

Yet still, she didn't feel as though she belonged there. She wasn't like them no matter how she tried to convince herself that she was. She didn't enjoy the group sex that they seemed to. She wasn't as sexually liberated as them. At heart what Jessica wanted was to be loved by Jon and to form a unit with him in which she could feel safe. But she suppressed her heart's desire for she wanted to belong. She wanted to be like them.

Not belonging was something Jessica was used to. She had learned that you have to work to change yourself if you want to fit in. You adapt. Jessica could adapt to anything. She would become whatever Jon wanted her to be if only he'd love her. She would learn to enjoy it the way he did, learn to want the same things.

She wanted to be perfect for him.

She held on for the time when he would see that he needed nobody but her. She would fulfil his every need, his every requirement.

He would be completely in her power. And so Jessica dreamed as, one afternoon, she lay, resting, on the bed.

She thought about what had happened the week before when she had been woken by a handful of masked men in short dresses.

Jon had gone away for the night 'on business' somewhere and Sophie had gone out with a girlfriend. Jessica had been left alone for the evening and had gone to bed early.

She had been confused by the loud voices in the dark bedroom, and frightened. The light had been snapped on and Jessica had found herself surrounded by five men wearing rubber masks and baby doll nighties.

She laughed now as she could safely see the comedy without feeling the fear that she had felt then.

Sophie had appeared and jumped on the bed with her. She had been drunk, or stoned, or both.

"We thought you might have been bored, so I brought some friends back to play," Sophie had said. Jessica remembered how her eyes had rolled in their sockets. She had been terrified. Jon wasn't there and Sophie was too stoned to be in control of the situation and Jessica hadn't gathered what the situation even was.

The men had looked ridiculous in their frills and menacing in their masks. She'd felt nervous and vulnerable, prone and naked.

Sophie had made a lunge for the sheet that Jessica had been clutching over her nudity. She'd thrown it on to the floor leaving Jessica completely exposed. Jessica had almost slapped her.

"Party time!" Sophie had yelled and Jessica had shivered in fright when the men had simultaneously climbed on to the huge bed with her. They had crawled around her like puppies. Two of them had latched on to her nipples and begun suckling.

Sophie had been rolling around the floor in laughter, a drug-induced hysteria.

Jessica hadn't seen anything funny.

"Lighten up Jessica," Sophie had said when she'd seen Jessica's sour expression." They just want you to be their mummy. Look." Sophie had then stood at the end of the bed.

"Children," she'd shouted with authority and clapped her hands together. "Come and suck mummy's pussy." She had lifted her dress to her hips and widened her stance. Two of the enormous babes shuffled down the bed and nuzzled each other for her cunt, like two calves fighting over the same teat.

"See. They'll do whatever you want them to. Try it."

Jessica had felt disgusted by them all, and felt shame for it. Sophie was so progressive and free, she was so uptight and prudish.

She had felt like the naive, small-town girl she was.

She had said nothing.

"Now children, go and lick mummy Jessica's pussy," Sophie had then ordered in response to Jessica's silence.

They did as they were told. Jessica had thrown Sophie a bitter glance.

"Funny, I never had you cut out for such a prude."

Maybe Sophie had known that that would get her?

"I'm not a prude. It just takes me a while to wake up," she had said while the 'children' were lapping at her.

"You can smack them if you'd rather." Sophie had suggested chirpily and demonstrated by spanking one of them on his bare arse.

Jessica had found it a far better alternative and the two of them had spent an hour slapping them and forcing them to stand in corners.

It had been hard work, but she and Sophie had giggled into the early hours about it.

Now Sophie poked her head around the bedroom door.

"Hurry up. I'm going to take you shopping."

Shopping? Jessica didn't have any money. Sophie must have read her mind.

"Jon's treat."

She smiled. He was always treating her. Drugs, jewellery. He often had a little something for her when he came home.

*

Shopping for clothes should have been an enjoyable experience. But instead, it turned out to be a nightmare filled with humiliation and frustration.

Sophie had the cash and she knew where to go to spend it. They visited some of the most fashionable shops in London. If only Sophie would've let her take charge of the cash. It was for her after all, from Jon. As it was, she felt like an orphan being clothed by her new rich Mother.

Sophie didn't ask Jessica once if she liked the garments she chose for her. She just told her to try them on, and then to parade in front of her. The clothes were bought or not on the strength of Sophie's approval.

Jessica was standing in front of a full length mirror looking at herself in a long, shocking-pink, wrap-around skirt feeling like a sulky child. They had been shopping for hours and Jessica was at the end of her patience.

This skirt felt like the last straw.

"It looks great. We'll take this one too," she said to the assistant

"I'm not sure about this one Sophie," she said quietly. She just couldn't bring herself to assert her opinion over Sophie's. What did she know about fashion? Sophie had made that point perfectly clear in her attitude that afternoon.

"You're joking. It's brilliant," Sophie insisted.

"It's a little uncomfortable though."

"You've probably not got it on quite right. Here let me." Sophie pulled her over and proceeded to remove the skirt leaving Jessica half-naked in the shop.

She felt stupid under the shop assistants' curious gaze as it was, but now she thought Sophie was purposefully humiliating her for her own titillation and Jessica felt she could do nothing to stop her because she might appear ungrateful. And she was indebted to Sophie.

"There. How does that feel now?" She smiled up at her.

"Much better thanks," she replied weakly. She couldn't force her to wear them.

When they got home, Sophie insisted that Jessica parade each outfit for Jon in the living room for which Jessica despised her even more. Humiliating her in front of shop girls was one thing but in front of Jon was another. Besides which, Jon didn't seem interested. He seemed preoccupied and distant.

Jessica put her arms round his shoulders and kissed his cheek.

"Thank you for my clothes. They're beautiful."

"No problem. My pleasure. Just look beautiful for dinner tonight."

"Who's coming? Ben boy?" she asked hopefully. She hadn't seen any of the original crowd for weeks and she missed them, missed the fun they used to have.

"No. They're potential clients. I'm relying on you and Sophie to convince them that I'm their man." He smiled softly. It always melted her when he did that. He was asking for her help. He needed her and she wouldn't let him down.

"Leave it to us," she said reassuringly and Sophie snorted and left the room.

"What's her problem? She's been weird all day," Jessica complained, hoping to receive some comradeship from him.

"She's pissed off because I've cut her allowance."

"I didn't know you paid her one."

"She does a lot of work for me. Get dressed. Look beautiful for me." He kissed her gently on her mouth. She almost told him that she loved him.

She suspected that he loved her too sometimes. Though he hadn't actually said so, she'd seen it in the way he treated her. He was always gentle and, unlike Sophie and her accomplices, he never humiliated her and only ever treated her with the utmost respect. And she adored him for it.

It was these moments of tenderness that justified the rest to Jessica. She considered herself to be in love for the first time in her life and she wasn't going to let go of it easily.

*

"It's eighty per cent," Jon informed his guests as he spooned a heap of creamy-coloured powder on to a piece of marble in the centre of the table upon which they'd dined.

The four men each dipped in their fingers to taste. The atmosphere seemed very serious and business-like to Jessica. She stayed quiet.

Jon seemed to be waiting for their opinion.

"Okay." They all nodded in agreement with the fattest of the men. The one that Jessica had been allowing to feel her up under the table all evening so as not to spoil Jon's chances.

"We'll sort it out tomorrow then." Jon said and began to separate the heap into furrows for consumption.

So that was what Jon did. It had only just dawned on her. It seemed so obvious now that she knew, the flat, the car, the clothes, the odd hours, the odd people. He was a drug dealer. It only served to make him darker and all the more desirable to Jessica.

"Ladies first," the fattest said to Jessica and slid the marble slate in front of her.

"Thank you." She stood and bent over the slate, careful to hold her hair back while she snorted her line with the fifty pound note that he had rolled for her. As she bent over, the fat man slid his hand up her skirt and pushed his thumb up her cunt. Jessica said nothing. This was for Jon.

She sat back down and she watched as the groper swooped up his line on his wet thumb and sucked the powder from it, grinning across his wide face.

Jessica was repulsed but she maintained her glassy smile.

The cocaine was consumed along with a couple more bottles of champagne and the party grew louder and more boisterous until someone shouted, "Shall we take the party upstairs?"

The suggestion was greeted with loud approval and Jessica felt herself being whisked up to the bedroom.

"Come on then dear, let's see what you've got under there." The men guffawed and giggled like schoolboys as they looked at Jessica expectantly.

Jessica looked at Jon who was leaning in the door frame. 'Please', she saw him mouth.

Please what, she wondered angrily? Please undress and let these fat slobs paw her? How could he ask her to do that?

The drunken guests began to hum *The Stripper* tune and Jessica felt herself boiling. She looked over to Jon again, more in desperation this time. He nodded to Sophie and she nodded back as he walked over to Jessica and slipped his arm round her waist.

"They just want a bit of fun Jess. Please do this one thing for me. I've never asked you for anything before have I?" He was speaking in a low tone while Sophie was stripping for the men to the sound of jeers and shouts.

"No," Jessica answered sulkily.

"This is important for me. You care about me don't you?"

More than he could ever know, she thought.

"Yes, very much." He took her chin and lifted her face towards him.

"And I love you Jessica." He kissed her deeply and tenderly.

Her young heart exploded and she was persuaded.

"Sophie will take care of you, I've got to sort something out. Cheer up, it might be fun." He kissed her cheek and left the room with a grin.

How Jessica wanted to believe that he'd meant what he'd said. She believed it enough to allow Sophie to undress her and have sex with her for the benefit of their small audience.

But now as she found herself tied, face down to an upturned chair in Sophie's semi-circular bath-tub, it was Chris she thought about. There were no doubts about his love for her.

There were jets of piss hitting her from every angle. She was grateful that so far no one had aimed at her face, though the hot stream that was pelting against her cunt was burning and she could feel a dribble running down her neck, which unless she kept her neck craned, might've dripped on to her face and into her mouth.

She had to concentrate on something else. She needed Chris. Why hadn't she phoned him?

They were laughing at her.

Refusing to allow the humiliation to consume her she bit down on her teeth and focused on nothing but the physical discomfort of being bent and bound to a wooden chair and only hoped she would be untied before her back broke.

Jessica wondered if any of them had pissed for a week or had they saved it all up for her. There was so much of it. It splashed yellow around her fingers and toes in the bottom of the tub.

She was glad they were all having such a good time.

Jessica was grateful for the curtain of hair that fell over her face between her and them. Peeking through the damp strands she saw the fat, laughing faces of the men who were now naked apart from their shoes and socks.

Jessica jumped, startled by a fresh spurt that hit her on the back of the head. Her hair, now wet, clung to her cheek and neck. Droplets of yellow piss dripped from her fringe on to her nose and ran on to her lips.

Jessica clenched them tightly together. She wanted to shout, *no more*, but was too afraid to open her mouth lest the urine should seep in and taste.

Jessica imagined herself as they saw her. Thin, trembling, pathetic. Tied up, ungainly, upturned, arse-ended, drenched in urine over a chair in a bath-tub. It was a sad picture and Jessica cried in pity and loathing of it.

She made sure no one saw because the only things that had to remain concealed were her feelings. So long as she could pretend that she was there because she chose to be then she couldn't truly be a victim, could she?

If Jon thought she was a fun girl with an anything goes policy, then that was what she'd be because that's how he wanted her to be; that's what he liked about her.

And Jessica liked to be liked. She had to become what he wanted.

That was why she hadn't contacted Chris. He was part of a rare reality for Jessica that would've threatened everything. He would shadow truth over her fragile pretence and Jessica didn't want to know about truth. It was, in her experience, always painful. Somewhere in the back of her mind she knew this was all fantasy, but to bring that to the fore would invite total collapse and she would lose any hope of ever having Jon in the way she dreamed. She needed to believe in her own truth.

So Jessica clutched precariously in her hands the thin strands that held her fantasy together and hid them from the unpicking that reality would bring to her world.

As the last drops of urine were shaken from the various penises that hovered above and around her, Jessica pleaded with a God that she knew wasn't listening.

God had never listened to Jessica.

God was a man.

Anyway, Jessica thought as she was being hosed down with the shower head, what right did she have to ask for help? She put herself there. Nobody forced her. Nobody had ever forced her. It was her fault and she had no right to feel anything but shame.

Jon reappeared and wiped her face with a sponge. He smiled and kissed her mouth tenderly.

"I'm sorry. I had no idea what they were going to do. You're an amazing woman Jessica." She thought he seemed genuinely sympathetic. She appreciated his kindness though she was sorry he didn't appear to notice her tears. Perhaps then he would've known to save her from herself and the horrors that she was pretending to be enjoying.

Instead, he moved out of the way to allow the fat businessmen to hoist her and her chair out of the bath and into the bedroom where they placed her roughly on to the floor and fucked her simultaneously in the mouth and arse until they had each emptied themselves of their semen into Jessica's various orifices.

She was numb. All the pain had left her. She was limp and numb and staring, seeing nothing.

Jessica was without rights and without power, a place she had sworn she would never be in again time after time. And here she was again.

It seemed that no matter what she did, what measures she took to ensure her safety, she always found herself back there, in the same situation over and over again.

As Jessica lay in bed that night, she decided that her life was a circular path. A loop tape.

One day, she thought, *it will all just stop*. And sometimes she yearned for the peace that day would bring.

cuddles

Sophie had left early that morning and Jessica woke to find herself alone in the bed with Jon.

For the first morning in ages she felt happy.

She snuggled in closer to him and pulled his arm over her shoulder. He stirred momentarily from his sleep to kiss her then drifted back into slumber.

Jessica thought how beautiful he looked in the morning sun with his black hair falling over his eyes. She stroked the lock back off his face.

He was an angel and Jessica loved him.

If only this was their bed in their house and it was years from then with Sophie firmly in the past, she thought.

She wished he'd make love to her. Push himself deep inside her while she clutched him to her with all her strength and whispered how she loved him in his ear. Jon hadn't mentioned his love for her again after that terrible night the week before. The one that she had barricaded from her memory.

There never seemed to be the opportunity to talk to him, she thought regretfully. Jessica needed to seek answers to all the questions that burned inside her like, how did he feel about her? Was he ever jealous when he watched other men with her? Had he ever wanted to just run away with her like she had with him? Did he think he could ever love her like she did him? How did he feel about Sophie?

She leaned over and kissed his face gently. She wanted him to wake up but she also wanted that moment to last forever.

She wetted his dry lips with her tongue and he opened his eyes.

"You all right?" he asked in a croaky voice.

"Of course I am. Why shouldn't I be?" she answered softly.

"No reason."

Jon stripped the sheet from them and rolled her on top of him. She kissed him hard, feeling passionate and horny. He kissed her back just as strongly and Jessica could feel his hard-on pressing against her thigh.

Jessica rocked her body against his and thought how different it felt to all the other times they had been together. This wasn't the slow tender caresses she'd come to expect from Jon. He felt strong, powerful, needy.

Jessica was excited. They would make love. She was sure of it.

She struggled to keep a handle on her own passions, not wanting to spoil it by making a single incorrect move.

She felt as though she was on the precipice of a breakthrough and the trick was to take his lead but make it appear as though the initiative was her own, leaving him with a sense of oneness; of having met his perfect match.

She had to contain her need to be fucked. Her needs were insignificant. They didn't figure in the equation. Her goal was to find out how she could best please him, then do it.

Jon didn't seem to be taking any sort of lead for her to take over. Maybe he wanted her to take the initiative after all?

Jessica wished he would just give her some clue as to what he wanted of her. He could've made it a little easier for her. Then he did. He pulled away from her and leaned over the side of the bed. He opened the divan drawer and pulled something from it. Jessica was curious, and then shocked as he presented her with a tube of KY Jelly and an enormous dildo around which was matted a mass of elastic.

She looked from the objects to Jon who looked uncharacteristically sheepish.

"Please Jessica. Fuck me." It was almost a whine.

Suddenly he looked pathetic sitting there on his knees holding the thing in both hands, like a supplication. Jessica swallowed her reservations and took it from him.

She began to unravel the elastic to work out how she was supposed to wear it. She felt embarrassed to admit that she'd never used one before. That she'd never fucked a man before.

Jon took it from her after a few minutes of watching her struggle and deftly arranged the straps so that all that was required of Jessica was that she simply step into them.

"Stand up," he said.

Leaning on his shoulders she stood and allowed him to direct her feet through the correct hole then he pulled the whole thing up to her crotch as though it were a pair of knickers. Then he sat back down and looked up at her.

Jessica felt utterly ridiculous.

It didn't even stand up properly. It hung there limply, reaching almost to her knees and as wide as her own arm.

If Jon hadn't have looked so earnest, if he hadn't have been wanking himself while he looked at her wearing it, then she might have laughed, loud and long.

As it was she had to bite the inside of her cheek until it bled in order to suppress with pain the bubbling giggle.

What was she supposed to do now?

Jon was now apparently lost to his desire. Like a man deranged he grabbed the end of Jessica's prosthetic cock and pulled it towards him. She nearly lost her balance as her hips gave way to his sharp tug.

Jon put her cock into his mouth and began to suck it. There was nothing in the world could stop the laugh that spread silently across Jessica's face as she watched his deep throat exercises. He was sucking and licking it with such a fervour that Jessica thought it was a shame that there was no one to feel it.

It seemed such a waste of energy.

With not a flicker of passion remaining in her body or a smattering of respect left for Jon, she felt stone cold. She was back to pretending.

She was very careful not to let Jon see her laughing at him. She knew what that did to men so she kept her head up and back.

What, she wondered, was she supposed to be doing while Jon was performing a frenzied fellatio on her rubber prick? Was she meant to be getting off on it?

He was now spitting on the moulded tip and smearing it over his face. Jessica put her head back again quickly as she felt another rumble of laughter building.

"Now," he said in an urgent breathless tone.

Now what, Jessica wondered to herself. Jon answered her question by pushing his face into the pillow and sticking his arse up in the air. Jessica thought he looked most attractive from that angle and waddled over to kneel behind him.

The dildo, much to Jessica's continued amusement swung from left to right with each step. She put her hand over her mouth to muffle the snort as she watched her enormous cock swing like an elephant's trunk. When it accidentally slapped against his backside, he gasped in passion, she in near-hysteria.

Jessica took it in her hands and pointed it at Jon's splayed anus, which Jessica noted had not been wiped clean after his last defecation, slaughtering what little remained of the magic and mystery of the man of her dreams.

She looked from his tiny inverted puckering hole to the huge rubber helmet.

No chance, she thought.

A part of her amusement and flippancy was to cover the frustration and disappointment she felt. Would a man ever turn out to be what she wanted them to be? Right at that moment Jon was no better than Richard and all the Richards before him. He was weak and needed a Jessica to dominate him.

What had kept her obsession with Jon alive and burning had been her inability to control him and now there he was pleading with her to take complete control.

A trickle of anger began to flow in Jessica's gut as Jon's cowering, quivering body knelt before her; as ghosts from Jessica's past began to embody themselves within him.

The smile left Jessica's face and was replaced by a cold hard stare. A thousand mile stare, her mother used to call it. A stare that saw everything and nothing.

She took the tube, removed the top and pushed the nozzle into the tiny stained hole in front of her. She squeezed the lubricant into him until it oozed out of him then spread the rest over the dildo.

She felt dangerously calm as she reached over Jon's head for the pillows which she knelt upon to give her the height she needed to enter him from the correct angle.

The only sounds were of Jon's steady heavy breaths and the muffled traffic noise from below the closed window. It seemed to Jessica that the whole universe was holding its breath, waiting for her to plunder the everyman kneeling before her.

She shuffled forward a little and taking the cock in her hands she pushed it against his tiny hole. Jon squealed as she got the helmet inside – maybe in pleasure or in pain, it didn't matter to Jessica. She pushed it in a little further, then back, and forward again, and back and a little further again. Another muffled squeal from the pillow.

Jessica watched the taut skin that screamed red against the pale pink of the rubber intruder. There was something about it that made Jessica want to scream. She knew what it felt like to have a tiny hole stretched by a battering ram.

She bit down and gave a hard and sudden push which gained her two or three centimetres further entry.

There was a loud cry but no protestation.

Jessica saw him in her thousand mile stare. A stuck pig, pink and squealing.

Who was he, this pig?

Jessica began to thrust back and forth and with each forward movement Jon became someone else, or Jessica became someone else. She couldn't be sure.

It was her father, her uncles, their friends. It was Richard. It was a market stall holder. It was two boys. It was a fat white businessman. It was Sophie.

It was her.

She was them and this was her.

The tears flooded from Jessica's eyes. Her ears filled with the sound of Jon's screaming and her own sobs or was it her screams and his sobs?

She crammed more and more into him, holding it with both hands near the entrance to stop it bending away from him.

Jessica was possessed and terrified.

There was blood seeping on to her fingers, turning the cool pink rubber a furious red and still she could not stop.

There was a word emerging over the top of the mayhem in Jessica's confused brain. It was Jon. He was reaching round and slapping her thigh.

The word suddenly formed meaning in Jessica's head. *Stop.* He was shouting for her to stop.

He was bleeding. She had hurt him.

Her stare suddenly coming in to focus on reality saw Jon.

Just Jon.

He pulled the rubber from between his legs slowly, wincing in pain as he eased himself off Jessica's weapon.

She remained still and silent.

Dazed and dumb.

Once freed he slumped forward on his stomach and Jessica sat back on her heels. The dildo lay still and dead between her legs, staining the white pillow with traces of blood and faeces.

Jessica stared at it, her head bowed in shame and disbelief.

Jon rolled on to his side and looked at her.

"Am I bleeding?" he asked.

Jessica nodded her head without looking up.

She was worried about what he was going to say. He would think her crazy and the worst part was that she thought he might be right.

"I'm sorry Jon. I don't know what came over me. I didn't

mean to hurt you." Her voice was small and weak and the tears began to spill once again.

Jon sat up, wincing as he did so and put his arm round her shoulder.

"For what? So you got a bit rough, don't tell me nobody has ever got rough with you before?" He spoke softly and reassuringly.

"Why didn't you stop me?" Jessica said through the tears which were rapidly becoming sobs.

"I did," he replied softly.

"Sooner," Jessica insisted.

"Because I liked it," Jon said.

"But you bled." Jessica couldn't comprehend that he wasn't angry with her.

"I always bleed. I've got piles." Jessica looked up at him and smiled.

"I thought it was Sophie who had piles," she said wiping her eyes.

"She's got them too. Sodomy's got its consequences I'm afraid."

Jon rolled away from her and walked stiffly to the bathroom.

Jessica unstrapped herself and pulling on a T-shirt, walked over to the window which looked out on to the park. She watched as an elderly couple shuffled along the path under a shared umbrella.

Old people irritated Jessica. They reminded her that time was always passing and she wouldn't be forever young.

"One day," their eyes taunted, "you will be like us, only you'll be on your own, without children or grandchildren. You'll have no happy memories to comfort you, nothing to show for a life time. Nobody will ever love you enough to want to grow old with you. Think about that young lady when you mock us with your pretty, young foolish eyes."

And they were right, Jessica thought with a bitter wistfulness, the acceptance of which somehow calmed her.

If that was her destiny then all efforts to avoid it were futile and unnecessary.

She watched as a young boy and his father tried to get their kite into the air. She shouldn't fight it any more, she thought. She should just accept it as her destiny. Suddenly the wind collected the kite and it flew. The little boy jumped up and down in glee, pointing at it as it swooped. Then it crashed against a tree and he cried. Jessica smiled cynically, she had known it would crash.

Jon emerged from the bathroom smiling.

"I'm off to see Ben. Wanna come?"

It was the first time he'd invited her anywhere with him and if it had come an hour earlier she would have been overjoyed at the opportunity.

But not now.

Now she wanted to be as far away from him as poss-ible. The fantasy had broken as all fantasies must sooner or later.

She shook her head and with it her melancholy.

"Oh Jon I would love to but I've arranged to meet a friend for lunch."

She hoped he'd leave it at that. She didn't have the strength to fight persuasion.

"Okay. Another time."

"That'd be lovely," she said and smiled.

Jon kissed her cheek and left Jessica with a familiar empty sadness.

Standing in front of the mirror Jessica wondered who she was. She hardly recognised the woman standing opposite. How sad she looked. How pathetic. How pitiful. How ugly.

'Help me,' the woman said to her and began to cry. Now the reflection was of a little girl, lost, abandoned, orphaned.

It angered Jessica. "Fuck you," she spat at it, "leave me alone."

Wherever Jessica went, no matter how far and fast she ran, that face followed her, haunted her. It would never allow

Jessica to find happiness or serenity and she despised it for that.

It was the tortured face of Jessica's tumultuous soul.

It was Jessica's secret from herself.

surprises

Jessica moved away from the mirror and moped around the house, picking up magazines and putting them down, flicking through the satellite channels on the TV, playing CDs half-way through unable to decide what she wanted to listen to and picking at food from the refrigerator. Jessica was bored.

She needed to find something that would block out her feelings. Something to deflect the dawning truth that she didn't know how to deal with.

Her obsession with Jon was fading fast, with nothing to replace it but fear and loneliness. She was trying to fight the truth that told her he wasn't what she'd envisaged him to be, because if she no longer wanted him then she had no reason to stay. And she had nowhere to go. It left her alone.

Why hadn't Richard called her? she wondered sulkily.

Until then she had been relieved that he'd left her alone, but now she was lonely and it made her cross that he hadn't tried to speak to her or get her back. Was that how much she had meant to him? Had she not even been worth a phone call?

She wished her mother was alive. She always did when she felt miserable.

She could phone Chris, she thought. He was always sweet to her when she felt depressed. But she hadn't called him for weeks and felt guilty. Would he want to see her now? She was a crap friend, she thought. She didn't deserve friends.

She sat on the window sill and stared out on to the street, allowing a tear or two to drip down her cheek. She wished that someone would look up and see her there. She wanted to be seen. It would validate her misery.

They would see a princess locked in a tower.

Jessica liked that image and acted it out for a few minutes, looking longingly through the glass at the freedom of other peoples' lives.

How ironic that she thought she was pretending.

She went upstairs deciding that she needed to go out and clear her head. She took extra special care over her dress and make-up and every time she looked into a mirror she wore a martyred expression, trying out several different ones until she found one that looked most appealing.

She would walk in the rain and allow people to see how miserable she was. She needed their pity.

If Jessica couldn't face reality she could always find a fantasy to justify her mood.

The truth was that now she had no goal. There was nothing to work towards, no reward for all her efforts.

But Jessica didn't want to know all that. She was an optimist. Her repulsion for Jon would be gone by the time he got home and everything would continue as normal.

She was just having an off day.

She tried on a few of Sophie's coats and selected a leather bike jacket that she'd always admired. She looked at herself in the mirrored dressing room. She thought it looked much better on her. Sophie was too old for it, she thought vindictively.

She slipped it off and carried it downstairs.

The phone began to ring.

Jessica made no attempt to hurry to answer it as she had had instructions from Sophie to let the answering machine record the calls to save Jessica having to take messages. Jessica was perfectly happy to follow the instruction. She had no aspiration to be Sophie's personal secretary.

As she descended the staircase she could hear a man's voice leaving his message which was indecipherable until she reached the bottom stair when she thought she heard her own name mentioned.

She hung the jacket on the banister and opened the door to the living room to listen to the rest of the message.

". . . got to help me out here Jon. Whores these days are getting so picky. What's the world coming to? . . . (laughter). Phone me the minute you get back and let me know. Don't let me down or these Japs will have my balls for sushi."

Jessica was intrigued and wondered if it would be possible to listen to the message and still leave the digital-recording signal flashing. Otherwise Sophie would know that she'd listened.

Jessica was burning with curiosity and decided she would be able to and if she couldn't then she'd make up some excuse.

She sat in the armchair beside the phone and pressed the play button. She waited for the machine to rewind.

"You have one message," it said and bleeped loudly.

"Hi Jon. Roger here. I know I'm not supposed to phone you but this is an emergency. I've got this group of Japs over for a couple of days that I'm supposed to be entertaining. Pervy bastards. Will your girl do dogs? Just joking. But if she would . . . whatever, I need her tonight Jon. Sophie too, if she can stay straight. They'll pay anything. I've tried the agency and they won't touch it, besides Jessica's perfect. You gotta help me out here Jon. Whores these days are getting so picky. What's the world coming to? Phone me the minute you get back and let me know. Don't let me down or these Japs will have my balls for sushi."

"That was your last message." Click, whir, bleep.

Jessica sat very still.

The silence rushed around the room, screaming in her ears. Her mind raced from one realisation to the next – like fruit machine wheels spinning and stopping, presenting different combinations of truth till finally it was there, in front of her eyes.

She was their whore.

A steel hand tightened a fist around her throat and another squeezed her gut.

There was rage and yet still clutches of disbelief. Had she got it all wrong? Sophie could be Jon's whore, but not her. She was special.

No she wasn't. He had fooled her into thinking he loved her so that she'd stay. Jessica had known, somewhere, but she had chosen to remain blind to the obvious. She hadn't wanted to know.

The tears flooded from her eyes burning in the furious red flesh of her cheeks.

"You bastard," she whispered through her teeth. Then again, "Bastard," howling this time like a wounded animal.

Overcome by her sobs and fury she slipped on to the floor and cried into the chair. Visions of the horrors she'd allowed herself to be subjected to by them flashed through her mind like stations on a fast moving train.

She saw it all. Every cock and cunt, every cutting word, every sick satisfied grin, every tender caress from Jon.

"You stupid bitch. Why didn't you see?"

Unable to contain her rage, she flung her fists into the back of the chair and punched it over and over, sobbing more and more loudly. She was shaking, lost to anything other than her towering hysteria.

All that existed was the pain she felt in her stomach and chest. She swiped her arm over the table sending the telephone, answering machine and a vase of dried flowers hurtling across the carpet.

And that was just the start.

He had tried to destroy her.

She had let him make a fool out of her.

She flung a glass at the mirror above the fire and both shattered.

Jessica was wild.

The coffee table turned on its side and splintered.

She had let him sell her.

A table sculpture flew through the television screen.

She had loved him.

She flung the drawers from the writing bureau at the stereo system scattering papers and documents everywhere.

She stood exhausted, panting through her sobs, in the centre of the devastation, and howled again.

"Why?" She screamed at the ceiling and fell to her knees amid the broken glass and loose papers.

"It's your own fault, Jessica." She sounded her own name in disgust.

"You trusted him. You trusted a fucking man." She twisted her hair around her fists and pulled hard.

"You asked for it." She felt her skin tear under her fingernails where she dug them into her upper arms.

It made a good dramatic scene, she thought. Then the pain, like a knife twisting, reminded her that it was all real.

Her head was throbbing. The scratches on her arm stinging. "Shit," she said when she saw that she was bleeding. She was going mad.

She ran from the living room and up the stairs. Her eyes glazed, vision blurred, she only knew that she had to get out of there.

The whole house began to loom in on her, oppressing her. Everywhere she looked reminded her of either sexual atrocity or Jon.

She took a large suitcase from the closet and lay it on the floor in the centre of the mirrored room. She began to throw Sophie's clothes into it. Dresses, trousers, shirts, shoes, underwear, jackets. She hesitated at the jewellery but decided she'd earned it and threw it in also.

She was taking what was due to her. He had made a prostitute of her and Sophie had let him, pretending to be her friend. She was taking her pay.

In the bathroom she swept the make-up and perfumes from the cupboards and shelves into a wash bag and threw that into the case also. A box fell to the floor and several hypodermic needles scattered around her feet.

Jessica knew they were Sophie's.

"That's what he wanted to turn me into. A junky whore, like Sophie." She kicked them out of her way furiously.

Satisfied that she had collected all she wanted, she closed the case and strapped it shut. She threw it over the banister and watched it bump down the stairs and crash into the front door.

She was ready.

But she lingered on.

What was she waiting for, she wondered?

She walked back into the bedroom and stood looking at the bed in which it had all started. In which she'd held Jon in her arms that morning. She could hardly believe that that had only been a couple of hours before.

How so much can change so quickly.

There was still a small part of Jessica that didn't want to let go of Jon regardless of what he'd done.

"What are you thinking?" she asked herself. "Don't you understand that he despises you. He never wanted you. It was all a plot, a game for them and you fell for it."

The rage was boiling up again.

She walked into the closet, welcomed by several full length images of herself in the doors. She thought she looked so ugly standing there. Ugly and pathetic.

"That's who you are Jessica. Can you blame him for hating you. I hate you," she shouted at her reflections before fleeing down stairs as fast as she could to retrieve a hammer from the tool box under the sink in the kitchen.

She would smash them. Smash them all.

Possessed, she flew back up to the bedroom and flung the hammer hard at the mirror on the far wall facing the doorway to the closet in which she stood.

It bounced off.

Furious, Jessica stormed in and gripping the tool tightly in both fists she swung at her reflection with all her strength. It smashed beautifully and Jessica crunched on the remains of the first reflection as she struck each of the rest with more ferocity than the last until they were all gone and Jessica felt safe.

She laughed a little hysterical laugh as she looked around at the carnage about her.

"Drama queen," she said and dropped the hammer into the shattered glass.

Feeling a little avenged, Jessica started to feel nervous. She could go to prison for the damage she'd caused. What if someone had heard the noise and reported it to the police? They could be on their way.

She had to get out now but where was she going to go? Chris's, she decided. There was nowhere else. But what would she tell him? Not the truth; she was too ashamed.

Jessica quickly stepped into the bathroom to wash her face and dab cream on her scratched arms to soothe the stinging. She had hurt herself lots of times before in anger. It was nothing unusual.

She looked terrible. Her eyes puffy and red, her cheeks stained with mascara, her hair matted and wet with sweat and the red from her lips smudged over her chin.

Jessica was careful to avoid the eyes of her reflection. She didn't want to know what they were saying. She'd had enough. Looking but not looking, she re-applied a little make up and tied her hair back, feeling a strange, almost eerie sense of tranquillity.

Without looking over her shoulder she went downstairs for the last time and into the kitchen where she went straight to the coffee tin in which Jon and Sophie threw their loose change. She emptied it on to the table and picked out the pound coins. Over fifty she guessed, pleased, and swept them into a plastic carrier bag.

Jessica thought she should call a taxi to take her to the tube. The case was heavy and she didn't want to be seen by Jon or Sophie on her way to the station.

The idea of seeing either of them again made her shudder. She picked up the hand phone in the kitchen and ordered a cab immediately, impressing a great sense of urgency.

Then she called Chris.

"Hi, thanks for calling. I can't get to the phone right now . . ."

"Shit," she said and waited for the tone.

"Hi Chris it's Jessica. I'm in trouble and I'm on my way over. I'll explain everything when I get there. Please be in." She replaced the handset and stood by the window to watch for the taxi.

She didn't have to wait long before it arrived and beeped its horn loudly in the street making Jessica cringe. The last thing she needed was her departure being trumpeted. She was feeling paranoid enough all ready.

She ran to the front door, slipped the leather jacket on, collected the suitcase and slammed the door behind her firmly without looking back.

She put Sophie's Ray-Bans on to hide her swollen eyes and dragged the case to the car.

"Want a hand with that love?" The driver got out and heaved the case into the boot.

"Phew. Going for long?" he said, struggling under the weight of it. Jessica hoped her smile would be answer enough.

"Thanks," she said and climbed into the back seat.

"Where to?"

"Richmond tube station please."

Jessica looked out of the window as they drove.

It was drizzling with rain and the streets were grey and bleakly empty. Like her soul, and her life, Jessica thought sadly.

"Horrible innit?" the driver said over his shoulder.

Jessica shut her eyes and grunted a reply.

It was only a short journey and within ten minutes Jessica found herself on the platform waiting for a train that would take her to Chris.

It was all over now.

She had learned her lesson: just don't trust.

She mused over the various reactions they might show on their return. She pictured their horror and smiled beneath her glasses.

The tube pulled in and Jessica stepped on.

She stood near the doors with her suitcase. She wasn't letting that go for anything.

She had earned every single item.

teasing

Jessica had been sitting on Chris's doorstep like a waif for about fifteen minutes when Chris returned. The relief was visible on her face as she lurched into his arms and burst spontaneously into tears which turned into heaving sobs. Even Jessica was surprised by their intensity.

Chris was stunned by both her presence and her greeting. But like the good friend he was, he just held her since that was all it seemed was required of him for that moment.

"Let's go inside." He spoke gently and his tone reassured Jessica that she was in safe hands at last. She wiped the free-running snot from her nose with the back of her hand and followed him through the front door and up the stairs to his bedsit.

"What's happened?" Chris pulled her down on to the two-seater sofa which unfolded to double as his bed at night and handed her a toilet roll. She tore a piece from it and blew her nose.

"You remember I told you about that guy I met at the party?" Every few words were punctuated with a sob, some of which were authentic.

"Yes."

"I really thought he cared. How could I have been so naive?" More tears and a dramatic pause. "He just wanted me to whore for him."

"What?" Chris said horrified.

"I heard someone leave a message on the answer machine asking if his latest girl was any good. He's a fucking pimp Chris and he was trying to suck me in. How could I have been so stupid?"

Jessica's pain was real and, even though she was only telling half the story, its re-counting hurt her.

Chris wasn't sure what to say so he just held her while she shook in his arms. What was important was that Jessica was distraught and that she had come to him. He would do all he could for her. He liked being her crutch. It gave him a sense of purpose otherwise devoid from his life.

"It's all right now darling. You're safe here." He was rocking her slightly and Jessica wasn't sure if she felt comforted or patronised by it but it seemed appropriate so she allowed herself to be rocked.

Jessica was confused between the pain she really felt and the pain that she was acting out for Chris's benefit; between the sense of having hoodwinked Chris into believing she was a maiden-in-distress and actually being one; between acting the well-made victim to hide the shameful truth that she really was a victim, a victim of her own stupidity as she saw it.

When the line between fantasy and reality becomes so diminished that it no longer discriminates between the two with any clarity you know you're close to insane. And today Jessica felt she was as close to it as she had ever been.

Sitting there, eyes wide and staring while Chris rocked her she could see what a camera might've seen. It was a good ending, she thought. Then fear shrouded her when she suddenly realised she wasn't acting. The film wasn't going to finish. There wasn't going to be any music or credits to free her from the frame. She was going to have to find her own way out.

Jessica wished she was smaller or Chris larger. She tried to coil herself up so that Chris would be able to hold more of her, only slightly aware that she was frightening him with her humming murmurs.

She was doing it to add to the character but she found the sound of her own voice humming with each exhalation strangely soothing.

"You need a drink," Chris said, needing one himself, and pulled away to get them one wondering whether or not he should call a doctor.

Jessica took her jacket off, then put it on again remembering her scratches. She wasn't sure if she wanted him to see them or not.

Jessica's character felt frightened sitting there alone on the sofa. Anxious and paranoid she looked around her fearfully, wanting Chris to come back and make her feel safe again. Then she smiled at herself. "You're out of audience Jessica," she said quietly but it didn't change the fact that she truly did feel frightened.

Chris returned with a half bottle of brandy unopened and two tumblers. He poured a generous amount into each, handed one to Jessica and knocked back his own in one gulp.

He sat looking at Jessica as she sipped from her glass and waited for her to become calm enough to go on with the story. There were all sorts of possible scenarios going through his head and the idea of anyone hurting Jessica made him furious.

"Did they do anything to hurt you?" he asked as cautiously as he could. Jessica had run out of prepared script and was too tired to improvise.

"Do you mind if we don't talk about it any more Chris. I'm so tired." She rested her head in her hands theatrically.

"Of course not," he said and meant it. She would tell him when she was ready and he could see that she'd been through enough.

"Let me pull the bed out and you can crash out for a while. Okay?" Jessica nodded. Her head thumped and her eyes stung from crying. Sleeping would numb it all, stop her mind from its racing thinking.

She slipped off her jacket and shoes while Chris turned the sofa into a bed. He didn't notice the scratches on her arms or he chose not to comment, either way he said nothing. She lay down and closed her eyes, smiling as he covered her with a quilt and kissed her forehead. She heard the sound of the curtains being drawn and soon nothing but the silence of deep sleep.

Chris sat in the armchair and watched her as she slept. He

thought she was the most beautiful and most disturbed woman he'd ever met. He felt so sure that if she'd just give him the opportunity, he would be able to help her. He'd love her to health. That was all she needed; someone who'd love, really love her. How could he tell her it should be him? He could cry for her, for the wasted potential. He thought Jessica could be brilliant which is why her apathy and lack of ambition frustrated him so. She wasted herself on one worthless relationship after another.

He sighed. No matter how hard he tried to understand her, he could not quite get a handle on why Jessica was the way she was and did the things she did. And he only knew a fraction of what those things were.

Jessica slept for a few hours and awoke to the smell of frying garlic. She opened her eyes and looked around the room which looked warm and pleasant in the orange glow of the table lamp and the bars of a small electric fire.

She must have been sweating as her T-shirt was wet through. She pulled it over her head and threw it to the bottom of the bed, then lay down again.

Chris was clattering about in the kitchenette which was set back into an alcove and sectioned off inadequately by a tatty curtain.

Tatty was how the whole room and everything in it appeared to Jessica, but tatty in a Chris way which managed to appear elegant too. There were crammed bookshelves, a paper-strewn desk, an expensive stereo, an Indian rug, framed drawings and prints covering the walls, and hundreds of small objects collected in baskets like the treasured contents of a small boy's pockets. Everything she knew about Chris was symbolised somewhere in the room. It was really his, she thought, and smiled.

Jessica was envious of his home. Why didn't she have a little home that she could make her own? The flats she'd had in the past had never represented homes, only passing places on a single track road.

She wondered what her home would look like if she had one – how she would furnish it, what atmosphere would adopt? – but all she could see was Sophie's home.

The lead weight reappeared in her stomach. Had all that really happened? She shook herself, annoyed. "Forget it will you," she whispered.

They say you can tell a lot about a person from the place in which they live. Perhaps Jessica was afraid to have a home in case it reflected some hidden design of who she was. It might give the game away and reveal the truth, whatever that was.

Jessica's home, if she had one in which to be reflected, would be empty and cluttered, bright and shadowed, modern and period, chic and kitsch, cosy and stark for she was a mass of confusing contradictions without a theme.

Anyway, Jessica didn't want to be tied down, she liked to think she was free and that house dwellers were envious of that. No, homes aren't for people like Jessica. Homes are synonymous with stability, responsibility, family and adulthood all of which are grown-up things that have no place in the lives of children.

She heard the kitchen curtain being pulled back on its rail and closed her eyes again. Chris was coming and she didn't want him to see her before she'd had chance to wash her face. She heard the springs squeak under his weight as he sat in the armchair and then the rustle of a newspaper being opened.

It was a pleasant feeling being semi-naked under the quilt with Chris sitting so close. She knew he fancied her and so liked to tease him sometimes. She found herself imagining the two of them having sex on the rug in the warm orange glow of the room. It looked nice in her head and she felt it in her cunt. She didn't really fancy him but in the circumstances she found the idea very appealing.

Pretending to be disturbed in her sleep she moaned and turned on to her back making sure she pulled the quilt down on to her ribs to bare her breasts. Now Chris would be looking at her, she thought, pleased. He would be horny. He would be wanting to touch her but he wouldn't dare.

The thought of him staring at her breasts and desiring her made her nipples harden and he would see that too.

Chris was watching and Chris did have an erection. He did want to run his hands over her body and kiss her nipples and her mouth and her pussy. He wanted it so very much but he knew that that wasn't what Jessica needed at that moment. It was the last thing she needed. She needed the support of a good friend and he loved her enough to give it to her without conditions so he rose quietly and went back into the kitchen.

Jessica was surprised and annoyed when she heard him leave. Didn't he want to look at her? Perhaps he didn't fancy her anymore? How dare he walk out on her gift. Perhaps he'd gone for a wank, she thought hopefully.

A few minutes later he returned with a cup of coffee. She felt him pull the quilt back up (to protect her modesty, she assumed) before waking her.

"Jessica," he said quietly. She pretended to stir.

"What time is it?" she asked with her eyes still closed.

"Seven o'clock. You slept for ages. There's a coffee down here for you."

He was being so nice that Jessica felt a twinge of guilt for teasing him.

"Thanks Chris. Have you got any cigarettes?"

"Yeah, sure." Jessica sat up and quickly brushed her fingers through her hair and wiped the make-up from beneath her eyes while Chris fetched them from the kitchen.

"How are you feeling?" he asked as he sat on the bed beside her and lit her cigarette.

"Hungry!" She smiled intent on changing the subject. She had no intention of discussing what had happened any further. It was behind her now and she would do her best to forget it. "What are you cooking in there?" she asked chirpily.

"Chilli," he replied, relieved that Jessica seemed somewhat recovered.

"Smells great. Let's eat."

Chris served the meal while Jessica freshened up in the bathroom which was across the hall and shared between two other bedsits.

She made the journey wearing only her jeans and holding one of Chris's shirts to her chest. She hoped she might bump into one of the neighbours so that she could look embarrassed and coy and thrill under their gaze. But she didn't and was disappointed.

More than ever she needed attention. Needed to know that she was desirable, that she was attractive and wanted. Jon hadn't wanted her but there were lots who would.

She took a quick shower and without drying herself slipped Chris's shirt over her wet body. It clung to her and the white cotton took on a transparent quality as her hair dripped water down its front.

He'll like that, she thought as she grinned in the mirror.

"You're not thinking of seducing Chris, are you Jessica?" she asked her reflection.

"I might be," she answered herself.

Collecting her clothes she walked slowly back across the landing back to the bedside.

"There weren't any towels in the bathroom," she said as Chris tried not to look at the flesh of her breasts through the wet shirt as she stood before him in the bright light of the kitchen.

"I'll get you one." His voice faltered and Jessica smiled to herself triumphantly as he fled from the kitchen. She'd got him that time.

Chris folded the bed away into a sofa and Jessica sat on it to eat her meal from a tray. He sat in the chair opposite with his tray and they chatted lightly.

Jessica found herself looking at him and seeing somebody quite different to the Chris she'd seen before. He seemed to have grown more handsome, more witty than she'd previously thought him to be. Maybe she did fancy him? He wouldn't treat her like a whore.

The more she thought about it the better it sounded. She could live here with him in his lovely home and start writing again while he worked at the restaurant and in the evening they would curl up and watch TV together or read favourite passages out loud to one another and later they would make love on the Indian carpet and crawl into bed and sleep with coiled limbs till morning.

A beautiful fantasy and Jessica could make it real.

Could she fall in love with Chris? Perhaps she always had been and just not seen it before. It was convenient to the fantasy that she did love him and so she decided she did.

It was as easy as that for Jessica. She has a need, imagines a route, then goes all out to get it.

Jessica finished first and took her tray into the kitchen aware of Chris's eyes, which were following her naked legs. She came back in and put a mellow compilation tape on the stereo, making sure she bent over far enough so that Chris would receive a full view of her cunt peeping out from under her backside.

Then she sat down again but this time she lifted her feet on to the sofa so that her knees were together under her chin and her ankles formed open curtains.

Poor Chris couldn't hide his blushes as he was confronted with Jessica's pinched lips. She could see he was having difficulty knowing where to look in his embarrassment, so she closed her eyes and rested her head back against the sofa, innocently pretending to listen to the music so that he could look without being caught.

Chris did look. Chris stared in disbelief. He needed to excuse himself to adjust his penis, which throbbed uncomfortably in his pants. But how could he leave this vision? How could he stay?

The idea of sharing a bed with Jessica in a few hours was

looming hopelessly and delightfully. He would have to lie there next to her with a stiff prick all night. What could be more terrible or more wonderful?

He resolved to relieve himself beforehand.

winning

Jessica was in her favourite role of seductress, vamp and predator and the more disturbed Chris appeared by it the more excited she became.

The night had already turned into the next day and the question of bedtime had been hanging heavily in the atmosphere for some hours. Especially for Chris who found his friend completely changed from the sad, sobbing chum who needed his care, to a prowling, threatening lioness intent on a kill.

Yes he wanted her, but he wanted her small and vulnerable and needy, the way he knew she truly was. This other Jessica appalled and terrified him.

Jessica had always slagged off the men she had slept with to him. He knew every nuance of male behaviour that she despised. He had great insight where Jessica was concerned and knew instinctively that if they had sex, he would become part of the problem instead of the solution he longed to be; that he would become an object of Jessica's loathing in the same way as every other man in her life had been.

He knew that getting in to bed with Jessica in this state would be like climbing into the jaws of a rabid dog.

Intent on her prey, Jessica was going to give Chris the best sex he'd ever had. She was going to lavish him with her tongue, tease him then slowly slide up and down his cock with her cunt clenched and while he watched her she'd perform a powerful orgasm for him, which would make him cum too. Then she would collapse into his arms and tell him how long she had waited for this time; how much she cared for him; how much she needed him. It was a tried and tested success formula in three easy stages and Jessica had few doubts about it working for her now. She was more than confident. It wasn't a risk because she'd always known that he wanted her and now she was going to let him have her.

Stage one.

"Shall we go to bed?" she said.

Normally Chris would've done anything to hear those words from Jessica's lips but now they chilled him to the heart.

"Yeah, sure. You must be tired," he said hopefully.

"Not especially. I just thought it'd be nice to chat in bed."

Jessica sounded casual and sincere and Chris relaxed a little. Maybe he was just being paranoid.

Chris pulled the bed out for the second time that day. He spread the sheet, threw on the quilt and Jessica jumped in giggling.

"It's ages since we've done this. I feel like a little kid." Chris looked at her in his baggy T-shirt and smiled.

"You look like one in that."

"What about without it?" Jessica said coyly and pulled the garment over her head.

Chris's breath caught in his throat and he almost choked on it. She was kneeling and naked and staring up at him, feigning the innocence of an angel only just belied by the Machiavellian glint in the blacks of her eyes.

Consumed by his desire he struggled for air. His love for her wavering weakly beside the baser instinct, while Jessica was exploding with the pleasure of what she saw in his eyes, and in his trousers.

His gaze of admiration was all the nourishment Jessica needed to revive herself. And she needed it now so very badly. The wound that Jon and Sophie had carved into her was deeper than even Jessica knew. It was a matter of survival. Survival and existence. That was Jessica's life.

"You look like a kid with tits," he said in an attempt to alleviate the tension.

"Bastard!" Jessica laughed and threw the T-shirt across the room at him. Chris ducked playfully.

"Well you asked." He threw it back at her and she dived beneath the quilt.

Chris was rather hoping that she would put it back on but she pushed it on to the floor instead.

Suddenly aware of his shyness, Chris turned off the lamp before undressing to his shorts and T-shirt and sliding in next to Jessica.

It wasn't a double bed so there was no avoiding flesh contact, but that didn't bother Jessica who wriggled childishly under Chris's arm and lay her head on his shoulder with her body pressing up against his.

Chris lay rigidly still as Jessica lifted her leg on to his and slid her hand under his T-shirt on to his stomach.

"You've grown a belly," she snorted and squeezed the flesh there. That wasn't all Chris had grown. He was now sporting a fully erect penis which he prayed Jessica wouldn't find.

"It's just my chest relaxing," he said. Jessica laughed loudly, louder than the joke was funny. She was excited, exhilarated, lost to the game.

Stage two.

She pulled herself up and leaned on to his chest. They were both silent and there was a sudden change in atmosphere.

Jessica stroked the hair out of Chris's face. He could only make out a vague silhouette of her head looking down at him. He swallowed nervously and his cock twitched involuntarily. If he was going to do something to stop this happening then it was going to have to be now. Now or never.

He felt Jessica's soft fleshy lips press gently against his own and her tongue wind itself around his and he knew the answer was never.

Jessica rolled herself on top of him and lay the full length of her body along his. She felt his erection pressing against her and she clutched it between the tops of her thighs and squeezed as Chris came alive.

He had lost to her; let her down; melded with the everyman

that was her enemy. But he wasn't to feel that until afterwards when lying in the aftermath of sweat and sperm; in the retrospective where all shameful feelings are felt.

For now losing was a joy as he kissed her hard and passionately; as he allowed her to push down firmly on his cock; as he watched her breasts bounce; as she buried him deeply inside her, as he watched the ecstasy on her face as she brought herself off and when he thrust his hips high into her and filled her with his sperm.

Then losing was the greatest moment in his personal history.

But now she lay limp beside him and he was no longer her friend but her enemy.

Who would save her now?

Jessica was pleased with her performance, her achievement, but what was that feeling in the pit of her stomach that felt so much like grief? Where had that void come from that felt so empty and stark in her chest? How was it that that old familiar desert of loneliness was upon her?

This is what she had wanted. Chris was going to be her future. If that was so then why was she cringing at his proximity and why did she want to be a thousand miles from the bed she shared with him?

Jessica couldn't afford to admit that she might have made a mistake. She didn't have the luxury of choice like others. Jessica could not, would not be alone. She would force herself to swallow her doubts and her grief because she needed his love. It didn't matter that she didn't love him as long as he loved her. She just needed to be adored and she knew she could be sure of that from Chris.

"Are you okay?" she asked him in a soft voice.

"Fine. Are you?" he whispered.

"Mmm."

Silence.

Chris was far from okay. He was furious with himself. How could he have been so weak, so selfish? He was scared for the future, picturing all the possible consequences of his weak will.

What right did he have to call himself Jessica's friend? He deserved anything she gave him.

It was Chris's turn to hate himself. He'd taken advantage of her when she was vulnerable.

"Want a cigarette?" Jessica asked him, reaching over him for the pack.

"Yes thanks," he said. His politeness seemed remote and misplaced. Both were uncomfortable and neither knew what to say to the other.

Chris watched Jessica's face light up under the flare of the match as she lit two cigarettes. Her innocence stabbed his conscience once again. If he knew nothing else he knew that he couldn't do it again. But how was he to tell her without hurting her.

Stupid bastard, he cursed silently of himself.

He took the cigarette that Jessica offered him.

"Thanks," he said and drew on it deeply, exhaling and sighing simultaneously.

Jessica had been too wrapped in her own thoughts to notice Chris's tension at first but now she sensed something wasn't as she imagined it would be. Why was he so quiet?

"That was really nice," she said. "I'm glad we did it. Are you?"

Silence.

"Chris?" Jessica felt panic rising in her chest. Why didn't he answer?

"It was nice but I'm not sure we should have." Chris's voice sounded small and hesitant. He so much didn't want to hurt her. He had never intended to hurt her.

Jessica smiled. He just needed some reassurance that she wasn't just going to dump him, she thought.

Stage three.

"I feel a bit embarrassed but I'm really happy Chris. I . . . I've wanted this for a long time but I never had the courage to make a move. I was scared that you might not want me," she lied.

The formula had proved that delicate male egos needed to be inflated and flattered and she had found that the uncertain adoring young girl was usually the best tool for the job. Even though she was getting a bit old for that role she figured that, because Chris was ten years older, she could still get away with it.

For Jessica the Chris of before had completely melted away leaving a man who needed to be conquered. That she needed to conquer.

For Chris, the Jessica of before was only reinforced by this new desperation he saw in her. The pain in his chest and the tears in his eyes told him that his fears were well founded. He knew she was lying. Had she forgotten who he was, that he was the man with whom she'd spent all those hours describing why she loathed his entire gender? They were gullible, flatterable, weak and predictable and now she was asking him to succumb to her folly or reject her.

Why hadn't he slept on the floor? He knew there would be no future after sex with Jessica.

Another tear — for he truly loved her like no one had ever loved her and now he was going to lose her. He could prolong the loss by going along with the game but that would be agony for both of them.

He owed it to her to tell her the truth.

"Jessica, you don't need this." His voice was firm but gentle. It put a fist in Jessica's stomach. She froze in his arms.

"I love you and I don't want to hurt you. And I don't want to see you hurt yourself any more." It wasn't coming out right. Chris struggled to find the words that would explain what he wanted to say.

Jessica remained frozen, waiting to hear the rest.

"What are you trying to say, Chris?" There was an edge of desperation in her voice, a hint of pleading. She uncurled herself from him and sat up with her back to him.

Chris put his hands over his face in frustration as he felt the distance that she had just made between them.

"I'm trying to say that I can't give you what you're looking for." He groaned at the inadequacy of his words.

Silence.

Jessica had begun to shake. This just couldn't be happening. Not from Chris. First Jon and now Chris. What was wrong with her? Was she so repulsive? How dare he turn her down. Nobody turned her down. That was her place, her prerogative.

"And what is it exactly I'm supposed to be looking for?" There was now angry sarcasm in her voice. She reached for another cigarette.

Chris flinched at her tone. He knew this would happen. He'd hurt her.

"I don't know ... something ..."

"What – clarity – Chris," she interrupted sarcastically.

"Please don't be angry with me Jess. I'm just trying to do what's right for both of us." It was Chris's turn to plead but it was too late to ask for Jessica's mercy.

"Don't patronise me. How do you know what's right for me?" Jessica felt hard and bitter and angry. The tears were rising and that made her angrier. Why could she never be truly angry without crying? It just made her look pathetic. She swallowed hard to try and gain some control.

"I'm sorry Jess. I really am." And he really was.

The tenderness in his voice destroyed the last vestiges of control over the emotional torrent that Jessica had been fighting back and the deep sobs of the morning returned with fresh ferocity.

"So sorry ... that you thought ... it'd be okay to ... fuck me? Hey Chris. Was that right for both of us? Did you ... have a good time?" She scrambled off the bed in a rage, frantically searching for the T-shirt to cover her vulnerability and her nakedness. She didn't want him to see her naked now, not ever. He had made her look a fool, made her think he wanted her and now she never wanted to see him again.

Chris was crying also but Jessica didn't see his tears in the dark. She was right. He had fucked her. She had every right to be angry with him. What could he say? He had no defence. He was guilty. He was shit and all he could say was that he was sorry.

Chris was disgusted with himself and afraid for Jessica. What would she do?

Jessica ran to the bathroom and locked the door. She slid on to the floor behind it in the dark and banged her head against her knees.

"Why . . . ?" she growled ferociously between clenched jaws, consumed with the same panic and terror of a wounded animal caught in a trap. Cornered and threatened, she fell on to the floor and punched it with her fists as reality rained down.

Jessica suddenly stopped her kicking and punching. Wretching, she vomited into the toilet bowl.

Sitting on the side of the bath-tub in the half-light that shone through the small square of glass over the door from the hall, she concentrated hard on breathing deeply until her sobs were under control: her sense telling her that she must calm herself, that the edge was a precarious place for her and that she must step back from it. She mustn't give way to the insanity that enticed her. She had to get a grip.

"Jess . . . Are you all right in there?" It was Chris.

He was worried about her, Jessica thought. Good. Let him suffer.

Silence.

"Jessica please . . ." Chris was scared by her silence. He didn't know what she was capable of doing to herself and his imagination was torturing him.

"For fuck's sake Jessica open the door." His impatience infuriated Jessica again.

"Just leave me alone Chris, go away." She wished she hadn't sounded so pathetic.

"No. Not until you come out and show me you're all right."

What did he think she was doing, committing suicide? She laughed sardonically and opened the door.

"Did you think I might kill myself over you? Sorry to disappoint you darling, but you're just not that big a deal." She smiled bitterly and slammed the door shut again.

Behind the door the brave cockiness melted into despair once more.

"Please talk to me." Chris leaned heavily against the other side of the door and Jessica thought she heard him sniff.

She hoped he was crying, hoped he was hurting as much as she was. She would make sure of it.

She flung the door open wide.

"I seem to remember you wanted to talk before, funny though it felt more like being fucked to me." She walked past him into the bedsit and began to pull on her clothes.

Jessica seemed to have conveniently forgotten that it was she who suggested they get into bed to talk, and that it was she who made the first move, that it had been her plan from the beginning. This way all she had to remember was that he had fucked her knowing that he didn't want her. He had used her, abused her trust and her friendship.

It simply went to prove that he was no different from any other man she had encountered in her life and therefore she was completely justified in despising him in the same way. The way he deserved. The way they all deserved.

As she tore around the room throwing her things into her bag, she could see him, sitting on the arm of the chair with his head down. She quashed the suggestion of guilt and shame she felt with the weight of his crime. Why should she feel bad when all she had wanted to do was to love him?

"Where are you going to go?" Chris asked gently. Everything was moving so quickly, too quickly; he didn't have time to think.

Jessica thought that was a good question. She had no idea

where she was going but she knew she had to be out of there, away from him, the new object of her agony.

"It's a little late for platonic concern isn't it." Jessica answered coldly. There was something in her that wanted to stay to abuse him, to tear him to pieces but the urge to escape was winning by a nose.

She buckled Sophie's suitcase and walked over to the phone. Picking up the receiver she said "Taxi number please?" to Chris without looking at him.

"Jessica please, it's four in the morning. At least stay the night." He stood behind her and put his hand on her shoulder. His touch had the same effect as an electric shock to Jessica and she shook him off with a violent shrug.

She turned back to the phone and dialled. Chris sloped back to the arm of the chair and watched her blankly. What had he done?

"Can you give me a taxi number for Lewisham please?" She replaced the receiver then picked it up again and called for a cab.

"Will you phone me in a couple of days?" Chris was panicking. She was going to walk out and he would never see her again.

"I don't know." Jessica knew she wouldn't but she felt the need to appease him, mainly so he would let her go without a scene. She couldn't bear the idea that he might beg.

"I'm so sorry Jessica. You can't know." She looked up at him for a moment. She knew he was and she could feel his pain as well as her own but there was no going back.

It was too late.

"I do know," she said softly. "And I'm sorry too."

The sadness of the reality of saying good-bye to the only friend she had ever had suddenly stung her and her eyes filled with a softer tear.

For that moment they were connected, knitted by their pain as each looked into the eyes of the other. They fell across the divide and clutched each other tightly enough to share the same soul. Each knowing they were losing something very, very precious.

A horn beeped from the street which struck fear and panic into both their hearts and they clung a little longer delaying the wrench.

Jessica pressed a kiss against his cheek and, without looking back, picked up her suitcase and ran down the stairs and into the street.

Almost blinded by tears she threw the case into the back seat of the cab and climbed in beside it slamming the door behind her.

She looked up to the lit first-floor window and the man that stood, framed within it and bled for the piece of her she'd left behind.

"Where to love?"

pass the parcel

It cost Jessica most of her remaining money to get her back across London. She went to Soho; the only place she knew for sure would be awake.

It was, but only just. The busy night was coming to a close as morning approached.

There was music drifting through brightly lit doorways, women standing in pairs and alone on the street corners and dark shapes shifted silently through the shadows.

Jessica was freezing. She ducked into the first open cafe. There were only a few tables occupied and Jessica headed for the table farthest from the other customers.

Trying to look inconspicuous is quite a task when you're struggling with a large, heavy suitcase that you can't seem to manipulate through the chairs and tables without catching them, causing them to scrape loudly on the tiled floor.

"Fuck," she muttered as a third chair made a squeak that set her teeth on edge.

Feeling sure that everyone in the cafe would be looking angrily at her, she kept her eyes low and sank heavily into a plastic chair at a plastic table and began to count the little money she had left in her pocket.

With her puffy, red tear-stained eyes, tangled hair, suitcase and the expression of fear and desolation that she wore, she might have been mistaken for a runaway if she hadn't been ten years too old.

She walked up to the small hatch and ordered a large coffee from a small, hard-faced woman who didn't speak but simply sloshed some thin brown liquid from a metal jug into a chipped mug and held her palm out for payment. Jessica gave her a pound and almost didn't wait for the change so withering was the woman's glance.

Back at her table, she tried to concentrate on formulating some kind of plan of action. She could go back to her family but even the thought repelled her. No, home was not an option, besides she hadn't been in touch for years.

Jessica's eyes drifted about the cafe and rested upon an old man sitting at the next but one table to hers. She thought he was the foulest being she had ever encountered but she was morbidly fascinated by him as he sat mumbling into his cup. His flaking skin was blotched red and black and he had what appeared to be years of encrusted snot on his top lip, which had matted into the long wiry moustache that was apparently growing from his nostrils. They had formed thin dreadlocks that hung beyond his bottom lip and Jessica shuddered in disgust as she saw him suck them into his mouth and chew.

He was totally oblivious to Jessica's sickened eye as he took a transparent bottle from the pocket of his weather-shredded coat and poured the oily liquid into his tea cup. Nor did he notice or indeed care that her stomach heaved as he lifted his arm to drink, disturbing the air so that Jessica received a full whiff of urine and methylated spirits. She put her hand over her nose and mouth and turned her chair away from him.

What about Richard? Would he allow her to stay with him for a while? A stab of guilt twisted in her ribs. How could she phone him after what she did. He probably still loved her though, she thought tenderly.

The thought of anyone loving her right then was enough to make Jessica adore them. Yes if he loved her then surely he would want to hear from her. Of course it would be painful but Jessica was genuinely sorry for her behaviour and she would do her best to show him that.

She'd give it till six o'clock then ring him.

The table that held the most fascination for Jessica was one around which a clutch of women sat, some of whom were girls closer to childhood than adulthood. Prostitutes, Jessica guessed.

Short dresses, heels and handbags, make-up and cigarettes.

They talked in loud confident voices and drank from small whisky bottles. Every now and then there would be a turnover. One would arrive and one would leave and take her place down the street. Jessica could see them through the window.

Jessica stared at them as discreetly as she could. She feared if she was caught there would be repercussions and being confronted by one of these women was the last thing that Jessica needed right then.

It was a strange feeling to suddenly find yourself homeless and in the company of tramps, whores and junkies. Divine retribution, she thought glumly, and forgetting not to drink the brown liquid in her coffee cup, she sipped from the lipstick-stained rim and her body shivered involuntarily at its nastiness.

She pushed the cup away from her as her nose wrinkled against the after-taste in her mouth, then pulled it back to her to warm her still freezing hands.

A tiny girl-woman in a scraggy velour mini skirt wandered over to the nearby table and joined the other women. Jessica was appalled by the thinness of her bare, wind-chapped legs. One rough brush against a table and she would snap in two for sure. She was welcomed by an older woman who put her arm round her and rubbed her back.

Jessica almost wished she could sit amongst them, be one of them, be rubbed and welcomed by them.

Jessica was consumed once again by the reality of what she was doing there in the middle of the night.

She pondered on the various reactions Richard might have to a phone call from her. The idea of going back to Richard sickened her slightly but she had little choice.

Did they all have a choice, she thought as she glanced up at the women? Nobody had any expectations of them; nobody really seemed to care what anybody else was doing. Yes, Jessica could understand what had brought them to this place. This was a society where nobody asked "What do you do then?"

Because everyone understands that you do whatever you can, a philosophy which Jessica understood well.

And they seemed happy, at least happier than Jessica but then that couldn't have been difficult.

Maybe it had been a good night for trade? Jessica thought, still musing over the plight of the women with whom she found it so easy to identify.

What constituted a good night? Jessica had lots of questions she wanted to ask. How many do you do in a single night; what do they ask for; how much do you charge; have you ever been raped; how did you get into it in the first place; what's the sickest thing you've ever done for money?

Jessica felt she could probably rival the latter without the excuse of being paid.

That stung.

"That's right, I'm a whore too." Jessica whispered into her cup. "How could I forget." She sank back into her self-absorption.

How could she expect to be loved and wanted by decent men. She was stained, tarnished. She was damaged goods and nobody would ever want her and she couldn't at that moment blame them. Jessica could hardly even bear the thought that she would have to live inside her own body for the rest of her life, never mind ask someone to live with her out of choice.

She was still confused by Chris's rejection. She had been so sure he loved her. Where had she gone wrong? Jessica was baffled.

Hurt, angry and utterly baffled.

And she missed him terribly. He had been her wailing wall and now it was all just rubble at her feet.

"Can I buy you a cup of coffee?"

Jessica looked up to see a man about her own age leaning over her.

Her first thought was what a mess she must look, the second was that he might think she was a prostitute and the third whether or not she should say yes.

"Thanks, no, I've got one," she said nervously. Then she almost leapt from her chair as another voice shouted from behind her.

"Oi! You'll do your filthy business out there, not in here." The thick Irish voice of the little woman boomed through the hatch and echoed around the cafe.

Jessica didn't know what she was more startled by, the enormous voice of the tiny woman or what she was implying.

The whole cafe fell silent and Jessica felt her face beacon with her blush as she became aware that every face in the cafe was upon her.

"Go on, fuck off the pair of you." She waved her arm towards the door.

Jessica wanted to say "But you don't understand, I'm not a prostitute, I'm a writer," but the woman was already making her way round to the front.

Jessica boiled in rage and humiliation. She looked back at the intruder who was smiling broadly at the fiasco.

"Meet you outside," he said and made his exit.

Jessica was scared. She was about to be thrown out on the dark street to where a man was waiting expecting something from her.

"You better move your arse, love," one of the women shouted over at her, laughing. Jessica looked at them, hesitating between the door and calmly explaining to the fearsome woman that it was a simple misunderstanding.

"Yeah, she's not messin'," said another.

At that moment the tiny woman came tearing round the corner with a conviction of physical violence in her eyes that made Jessica's decision for her. The dangers of the streets were kids' stuff compared to what this tiny furious woman threatened. And so, clutching her suitcase, she fled the cafe and the furious glare of her tormentor and the high-pitched cackles of laughter.

She did not look round as the little woman yelled "fucking tart" down the street after her, nor did she meet the eye of the punter that leant against the wall just outside looking to buy her wares, but rather lifted her head in an attempt to regain her dignity and began to stride purposefully along the street.

It was too much to hope that the man would not follow her and so, when he pulled her arm to stop her marching, she was prepared.

"What's in the case? Kinky stuff?" he said in a strong Midlands dialect.

Jessica instantly felt superior and put on her poshest accent with which she hoped to convince him that she was not a prostitute.

"Look, I'm not what you think I am, nor have I ever been. You've just got me thrown out of a cafe and I think the least you could do is leave me alone. Okay?" Jessica tried her best to look down at him from her fully extended five feet five and three quarter inches.

"Don't mess with me you fucking stuck-up little bitch. My money not good enough, is it?" He was standing dangerously close and he tightened his grip on her arm. If he was trying to frighten her then it was working.

"If you don't let me go in three seconds I'm going to start screaming," she said in calm, low, threatening tones.

Pressure, it would seem, worked well for Jessica. She'd never been so assertive in her life.

"Fuck you then," he said and turned with a shrug of his shoulders. And then, more to himself, "A frigid fucking whore!"

Jessica began her march again, shaking in disbelief. Narrow escapes were not a regular occurrence for Jessica. She rarely escaped anything and for a second or two she felt grateful.

"That was some achievement Jessica, getting thrown out of a cafe whose main clientele are whores and tramps," she said, the sound of her own voice making the voyage to nowhere seem more lonely.

At least the dawn was coming. Night was always a lonely

place at the best of times and these were certainly not the best of times.

The reaction to her close shave and the humiliation of her expulsion was delayed. Ten minutes later and some distance away the tears began to well. It was so unfair. Didn't they see how upset she was? If they had known what she'd been through would they have still treated her that way? Probably, Jessica thought.

The world seemed an angry, cruel, selfish place. Nobody cared that she was homeless and freezing, or that others were, she thought, as she trudged past the human bundles of blankets and newspapers that huddled in various shop doorways and brick alcoves.

But Jessica's pity didn't stretch too far outside of herself. For whatever reason these others lived the way they did, she was sure she could not. She wasn't strong enough. She was weak and spoiled.

Jessica crossed the road and headed for the phone box she saw there.

"Please be working," she said as she approached it. She lifted the receiver and encouraged by the dialling tone, shoved the case through the door and sifted through the loose change in her pocket for a coin.

Jessica shook with cold and nerves. What was she going to say? She pushed her coin in the slot and dialled the familiar number that used to be her own.

It rang.

Jessica's heart was beating loudly and she cleared her throat in preparation. The phone was downstairs and the bedroom up and Jessica feared that he might not hear it. She clung on and listened intently as though she might hear him waking between rings.

Her mouth was dry. She fumbled for a cigarette hoping she'd get it lit before he answered.

"Yeah?" Jessica jumped. It was him.

"Richard ... it's Jessica." She held her breath. There was a long silence then a sigh.

"I'm sorry for waking you up," she said, feeling the need to break the silence.

"What do you want Jessica?" It was a voice that Jessica was unfamiliar with. Its coolness hurt her. It knocked her off balance. And he'd called her Jessica instead of the pet abbreviation that she used to loathe. How she longed to hear him call her "Jess" now.

"I had nowhere else to go. I'm sorry." She began to cry which also met with silence.

"I've been walking the streets all night trying to find a way to tell you that ... (dramatic pause) ... I'm so sorry Richard ... for everything. I never wanted to hurt ..."

"Beepbeepbeepbeep" The money was running out.

"Shit." Jessica managed to catch it just in time. But she'd lost her drift in the panic. 'I'm sorry Richard, what was I saying' didn't seem appropriate somehow.

"Can I come round to the house?" Jessica asked in a soft persuasive voice.

A few more sighs.

"Please Richard. We need to talk." She pleaded with his silence.

"Fuck off Jessica," he replied in a weary just-leave-me-alone kind of way and the line went dead.

Like a soldier shot, Jessica felt the pain but couldn't quite believe she'd been hit. She stood stock-still in the glass box, the receiver still to her ear, listening to the tone of a cut off line – Jessica's life line.

Too shocked to cry. Too hurt to be angry. Overwhelmed by the void that had just swallowed her universe, she sat down on the edge of her case weak with fatigue and horror. Had she hurt him that much?

It was all Jon's fault. If he hadn't tricked her into thinking that he cared for her she would never have left him.

Her mind traced over her time with Richard. He had loved her and she had been so cruel. All he had wanted was to take care of her and she'd thrown it all away for a bastard who had effectively ruined her life.

Burying her head into her arms she began to sob. She cried in grief for Richard and for Jon and Chris, even for the men that went before. Suddenly she loved them all, wanted to be with them all. Curled up in a warm bed with all of them, loving her, wanting her. And now they despised her, knew her for what she was; a lying, selfish little bitch with nothing to offer anybody except pain.

She had deserved what Jon and Sophie did to her. She had had it coming. This was her punishment.

"Are you satisfied now!" Jessica said furiously through her sobs up to the sky. The wrenching sadness tore through her soul.

Jessica was too absorbed by her grief to notice the police car pull up alongside her glass house.

"Come on love you can't sleep here," a deep voice said. Through her tears, Jessica looked up at the uniformed man standing next to her.

"I wasn't trying to," she said more abruptly than she meant to. She was annoyed that he could make such an absurd suggestion. Did she look like a tramp?

"I don't care what you're doing, you can't do it here," he said unsympathetically and lifted Jessica by her arm which she snatched away. "I'm going for God's sake."

The police car trailed her for a little while much to Jessica's fury. Didn't she have enough to deal with without being harassed. Eventually it left her alone to her maudlin wandering.

The edge of night had lifted slightly and was slipping into dawn when Jessica came to the market place. It looked unfamiliar so early in the morning. It was busy with early starters, bakers delivering to cafes, men carrying crates of milk, waiters sweeping around tables and setting chairs, canvas tarpaulins being thrown over scaffolding and car boots being emptied on to trestle tables.

Jessica felt like an alien in the midst of this mundane activity. She was surprised to find that the world was acting as though nothing had happened. Didn't they know that she'd been through her own Armageddon? A minute's silence would've been nice, she thought, resentful that no one acknowledged her pain.

And then something caught her eye in the distance that stirred her from her stupor and suddenly Jessica was very much awake.

Bobbing into a cafe she slipped unseen into the ladies toilet where she washed, brushed, changed and made up her face which needed considerably more attention than usual.

There she was again, staring back at Jessica from the wall as she applied her mascara. She looked more sad than angry and the pitiful expression she wore irritated Jessica.

"Got a better alternative?" she challenged her reflection then stood back from it. "That's as good as it's going to get," she added with a sigh.

The day had grown lighter when Jessica emerged back on to the street, though the same could not have been said of her heart. With each step that brought her closer, her spirit died a little more.

She walked through the maze of hut-like constructions, past their shouting dwellers and stepped over the boxes of as yet undisplayed wares as her head screamed no to her feet which walked on regardless.

She was so close now that she could almost smell him. He hadn't seen her, not yet but he would soon. He was alone. That was good. She took a deep breath and practised a smile.

Her face felt taut and she realised her teeth were clenched tight in resolution. She could turn back if she did it now.

Turn back to what?

"Hi!" she heard her voice say confidently. The tall man turned round to face her. He studied her for a few seconds while she smiled at him.

Had he forgotten who she was? It was a possibility she hadn't taken into consideration.

"Nicest piece of cunt you ever had. Remember?" Jessica forced a flirty grin.

The man smiled a sickly smile.

Recognition, thank God.

"It's a bit early for shopping isn't it?" he said and leered at the breasts which Jessica was pushing out at him.

She stepped up closer and leant back against his trestle table, arching her pubic bone forward to form a small hill above her thighs.

"I like markets and I like mornings," she said without any subtlety whatsoever.

There was no place for subtlety in matters of survival.

The man stood between her open legs and leant over her, supporting himself with one arm on the table, the other on Jessica's crotch.

"Where's your boyfriend?" he asked and squeezed her cunt.

"I get bored easily," she replied.

"You won't get bored of me," he said with the same cockiness that Jessica remembered.

She had him wrapped around her finger.

It was all too short a step from there to the little makeshift changing cubicle where Jessica found herself being pushed on to her knees, eye-level with the large hands that unzipped the fly in front of her.

The fact that his penis wasn't huge did nothing to compensate for the way Jessica felt as he held her head with one hand and rocked his solid cock back and forth, in and out of her mouth.

She held firmly on to his hips for some control but she could not stop him from occasionally jabbing it into the back of her throat, just as she could not stop herself from retching when he did.

Nevertheless, he had restored her faith in the inanity and stupidity of manhood and Jessica was beginning to feel a little better as a flicker of her old superiority returned.

ORIGINAL
Ringpull

Every Mother for Himself

ED JONES

The Newfoundland Old People's Home means different things to different people.

To Jed Green, it's a marvellous (or so he thinks in the beginning) investment for the ill-gotten gains he kept secret from the tax-man when he went bankrupt. Also, it gives him the excuse to pop in and talk to the intriguing new nurse at the home. To Miranda, the new nurse at the home, it's a job she enjoys. Also it gives her access to the medical cupboard which, for a junkie, is important, especially when she can't always find the time to earn money from prostitution. To the attractive Charity Green, bored with her life and her dull marriage to sexless Jed, it's a chance to run a profitable business and to enjoy herself in the evenings with Miranda. And to the old people it's war when some of them start disappearing in the night. Dotty as they are, even the residents begin to wonder what exactly is going on in the cellar.

"Anyone who can make God working behind the counter in a chip shop seem absolutely normal, is bound to go on to greater, more outlandish things."
GINA MORRIS on *Come Again!* Ed Jones' first novel

IBSN I 898051 13 5 Available: *Sept 1994* **£8.99**

Ringpull

ORIGINAL
Ringpull

bitches &
bastards
angels
& saints

Michael Robinson

Royston Bone, Private Eye, is the *baddest* lover in town but what kind of
detective has nothing to detect? His first client, Dexter Humpage, gives him a
case that looks too good to be true - a missing person who just happens to
be living with Royston's ex-lover, Roxanne Bliss. But Dexter Humpage is
looking for more than a missing person- he's convinced the sassy Nadene is
the woman to cure his seven month bout of impotence. That is if she doesn't
take up Roxanne's offer and turn dyke. Meanwhile young Johnny Hammer is
lusting after pneumatic pin-up Lickie Loose. And when Lickie is kidnapped by
East End villains and held in an isolated cottage in Epping Forest; Johnny,
Dexter, Nadene, Roxanne, Royston, Robin the Rottweiller (Johnny's dog) and
a bundle of others find themselves caught up in a crazy white-knuckle ride of
amorous adventure and criminal activity.

Michael Robinson has re-cut the ripping yarn for the Nineties and produced a
speedball of a novel where low brow culture meets high brow literary
dexterity and the two get on like a house on fire.

"**Bitches & Bastards, Angels & Saints is the only candidate for the
soul kiss of life. This is one rude read that leaves the language
swooning in its wake - beautiful.**" JULIE BURCHILL

!BSN 1 898051 05 4 Available: Sept 1994 **£8.99**

Ringpull

Ringpull Order Form

All Ringpull books are available from good bookshops but may also be purchased by mail-order.

ISBN	TITLE	AUTHOR	PRICE	NO REQ'D	£ TOTAL
1 898051 02 X	**Come Again**	Ed Jones	£5.99		
1 898051 00 3	**The Baby War**	Peter Whalley	£5.99		
1 898051 01 1	**Death Duties**	Julian Roach	£11.99		
1 898051 18 6	**The Allegation**	Peter Whalley	£14.99		
1 898051 06 2	**A Matter of Chance**	Sheila S Thompson	£13.99		
1 898051 04 6	**Robbers Bandits Villains**	Peter Whalley	£7.99		
1 898051 03 8	**Vurt**	Jeff Noon	£7.99		
1 898051 05 4	**Bitches & Bastards, Angels & Saints**	Michael Robinson	£8.99		
1 898051 12 7	**Beautiful Soup**	Harvey Jacobs	£8.99		
1 898051 14 3	**Technicolour Pulp**	Arty Nelson	£8.99		
1 898051 13 5	**Every Mother for Himself**	Ed Jones	£8.99		
1 898051 10 0	**Jessica Likes It**	Tiffany Quin	£8.99		
1 898051 08 9	**Without Consent**	P Mantle & C Nagaitis	£16.99		
1 898051 11 9	**Pollen**	Jeff Noon	£14.99		
1 898051 09 7	**Purely Decorative**	Michael Montrose	£13.99		
1 898051 16 X	**The B Book**	Brian Randall	£16.99		
1 898051 19 4	**Mythtaken Belief**	Graeme & Sue Donald	£15.99		
1 898051 07 0	**Manly Stanley & the Killer Whale**	Ed Jones & R Jeffers	£9.99		
1 898051 17 8	**The Story of Ax**	John Perkins	£9.99		
			TOTAL:		

PLEASE SEND THE BOOKS I HAVE MARKED ABOVE.

I enclose £ .... PLEASE SEND CHEQUE ONLY, NO CASH to: Ringpull Press, Queensway House, London Road South, Poynton, SK12 1NJ, UNITED KINGDOM. Tel 0625 850037. All prices and publication dates are correct at time of going to press but are subject to change without notice. All orders are supplied at price on receipt.

NAME:
....
ADDRESS:
....
....
....
....

SIGNED:
....